CHARLES
in charge

Elizabeth Faucher

SCHOLASTIC INC.
New York Toronto London Auckland Sydney Tokyo

No part of this publication may be reproduced in whole or in part, or stored in a retrieval system, or transmitted in any form or by any means, electronic, mechanical, photocopying, recording, or otherwise, without written permission of the publisher. For information regarding permission, write to Scholastic Inc., 730 Broadway, New York, NY 10003.

ISBN 0-590-33550-2

Copyright © 1984 by Scholastic Inc.
All rights reserved. Published by Scholastic Inc.
All photos courtesy CBS.

12 11 10 9 8 7 6 5 4 3 2   5 6 7 8 9 / 8
                                          01

Printed in the U.S.A.

Chapter One

Check the notice board, the housing office had said. Maybe you'll find something less expensive.

Charles had nodded, trying not to look as disappointed as he felt.

We really *are* sorry, they said.

He nodded.

The notice board was in the Student Center, between the bookstore and the cash cafeteria. Charles dropped his suitcase and duffel bag, letting the knapsack and typewriter case fall more slowly. The lobby was crowded with other freshmen, all of them noisy and enthusiastic, wearing shorts and t-shirts that showed off summer tans. Not quite the academic atmosphere he'd anticipated. *Nothing* about Crawford College was quite what he had anticipated — especially his financial aid package.

He sighed, turning to examine the board. It was covered with mimeographed notices about campus activities, and he paused at the one announcing cross country team tryouts, then looked beyond it. Sports were okay in high school, but

1

once you started college, it was time to get serious. He glanced back at the tryout sheet, then down at his duffel bag where he'd packed his New Balance running shoes. Get serious. He studied the ads instead, most printed neatly, the others scrawled on the regulation file cards.

'75 MUSTANG, NEEDS WORK, BEST OFFER. CALL MATT, DELTA UPSILON.

ROOMMATE, M OR F, FOR OFF-CAMPUS APARTMENT, $150.00 PLUS UTILITIES. With a part-time job, he could maybe swing it — but not if he wanted to eat. And since he was hungry *now*, he would never make it until Thanksgiving break.

LOST — SILVER CHARM BRACELET, GREAT SENTIMENTAL VALUE, REWARD.

FOR SALE: SALOMON SKI BOOTS, MEN'S SIZE 9, LIKE NEW.

So far, not so good. A file card in red magic marker, the handwriting almost calligraphic, caught his eye.

WANTED: AU PAIR. LIVE-IN COMPANION/BABYSITTER FOR OLDER CHILDREN WHILE PARENTS WORK. OWN ROOM, PLEASANT NEIGHBORHOOD, WALKING DISTANCE TO CAMPUS. CALL 555-9385 FOR INTERVIEW.

Now *that* had possibilities. No mention of a salary, but with room and board, and the money he'd earned this summer at Pizza Hut. . . .

"Sounds excellent, doesn't it?" a voice behind him said.

Charles turned, seeing a guy with blond, curly hair and a big grin. Mr. California. He was wearing faded Levis and a LaCoste shirt that had probably been dark green when he bought it; a rucksack was draped over his left shoulder.

"Hi." The boy held his hand out. "I'm Buddy."

Charles shook it. "I'm Charles."

"Freshman?"

Charles nodded.

"Me, too." Buddy hefted the rucksack. "What do you think, I pass for a junior with this?"

"High school or college?"

Buddy laughed. "College, son. College."

"Oh," Charles said and took out a pen, copying the phone number for the au pair position onto an empty file card.

"Hey, wait a minute," Buddy said. "Thought you were after the Firebird."

Charles shook his head. "Need a job — my housing didn't work out. This au pair thing sounds okay."

"Some of my favorite things come in pairs," Buddy said solemnly, and Charles stopped writing to watch two extremely attractive girls walk by. "Wow," Buddy said when they were gone. "You ever seen so many legs in your life? College is *great*."

Charles laughed.

"Tell you what." Buddy draped his arm around Charles' shoulders. "By Christmas, you and me are going to go out with every single girl in the class."

"There are over five hundred."

"Yeah," Buddy said. "And that's just the *freshmen*."

Charles put the file card in his pocket. "Buddy, I kind of get the feeling you have a one-track mind."

"Yeah, but it's the *right* track." He gestured towards the bulletin board. "What's this au pair stuff, anyway?"

"It's French for helper. Some family's advertising for a live-in babysitter. I thought I might try for it."

"What?" Buddy stared at him. "You're kidding, right?"

Charles shook his head.

"But this is *college*! You don't want to be stuck with some *family*."

Charles shrugged. "Doesn't sound so bad to me."

"Wait a minute. This is humor, right? We wait eighteen years to get away from parents, and you want to go right back?"

Charles frowned uncertainly. "Well — "

"Look, what dorm you in?"

"I'm not."

"Oh, right." Buddy studied the luggage on the floor, then looked up, animated again. "I got it! You can crash in our room, no problem. We'll have some Cokes, I'll talk some sense into you — it'll be great!" He picked up the suitcase and typewriter. "Let's go."

"Yeah, but — don't you have a roommate?"

"Who, Martin?" Buddy was already walking away. "He won't care. I mean, the guy is out to lunch. First thing he unpacked was his Bunsen burner."

Charles grinned. "Pre-med?"

Buddy grinned back. "What else?"

Martin was alphabetizing and categorizing his books, so Buddy took some Cokes from the small

4

refrigerator in the corner and gestured for Charles to follow him. Seeing a pay phone in the hall, Charles paused.

"I'm going to make a call, okay?" he said.

Buddy shrugged affirmatively, popping the top on one of the cans.

Charles put some change in the telephone, checked his file card, and dialed. A woman answered on the second ring.

"Um, hello?" Charles cleared his throat. "I'm calling about the ad you put up."

No response.

"In the Student Center? At Crawford?"

"Oh, of course," the woman said, obviously surprised. "Are you a student?"

"Yes, ma'am. A freshman."

"And you understand what this sort of job will entail? I mean, insofar as your social life is concerned."

That sounded ominous. "Yes, ma'am."

"Well, then. I'm Jill Pembroke, and my husband and I will be interviewing on Sunday afternoon. Let me give you the address."

When he hung up, Buddy looked over his shoulder.

"Ten Barrington Court, huh?" He shook his head. "Sounds pretty suburban."

"I don't know, she sounded okay."

"'F'you say so." Buddy moved away from his shoulder. "You're pretty tall. You play hoop?"

Charles grinned. "Is that anything like basketball?"

"A little." Buddy flipped him a Coke. "Come on, I know a great place to hang out."

They ended up under a large tree next to the dorm, slouching in the grass, watching what Buddy described as "the most excellent girls on campus." Judging from some of the people passing by, he was right.

"Everyone always call you Charles?" Buddy asked.

Charles nodded.

"No Chuck?"

Charles shook his head.

"Not even Chas?"

Charles laughed. "No."

"Huh." Buddy drank some of his soda. "Not even *Chip*?"

"Not even."

"Huh." Buddy thought about that. "What're you majoring in?"

"International economic biophysics."

Buddy stared at him. "You gotta be kidding."

"Yeah." Charles picked a handful of grass, tossing the blades one by one. "I don't know. They say you don't have to decide until what, sophomore year? I guess I'll just take a lot of different things and see what I like." He dropped the rest of the grass in his hand. "What are *you* majoring in?"

Buddy shrugged. "My father likes us to be lawyers."

"Us?"

"I've got two brothers and a sister."

"Are any of them lawyers?"

"No." Buddy grinned. "I don't know, figure I won't start worrying until senior year, at least."

"Your father's going to love that."

"Yeah." Buddy stretched, finding a more com-

6

fortable position. "I don't know, he'll get over it."

Charles nodded, and they watched some girls walk by on their way to the dining hall.

"That's one thing that'll be different here," Buddy said, indicating the short sleeves. "Where I live, it's *always* summer."

"So, why didn't you go to USC or someplace?"

"Parents."

Charles frowned. "You mean, they made you?"

"No. I came here to be *away*."

"You don't get along with them?"

"We get along fine," Buddy said. "But this is *college* — I don't want my parents around. This is parties, and meeting girls, and — "

Charles laughed. "What about classes?"

"What about 'em?" Buddy gestured expansively with his Coke. Too expansively. "College is for fun." He paused, wiping the spilled Coke off his shirt. "My brother went here — I know this stuff."

"Yeah, well, I'm here to study," Charles said.

"This is *college*. No one studies."

"So, I'll be the only one."

"That's for sure." Buddy looked at him thoughtfully. "You always wear a tie?"

"Well — I don't know." Charles touched the knot, feeling self-conscious. "We're supposed to be adults now."

"Not until graduation."

"So you're going to spend four years just playing around?"

Buddy thought about that, then grinned. "Yeah."

They sat under the tree for a long time. Other

freshmen kept passing; Buddy exchanged noisy hellos with a surprising number.

"How come you know so many people already?" Charles asked.

"I went to matriculation. You know, that ceremony they had on the quad this morning?"

Charles nodded. "I didn't get here in time."

"Do your parents know your housing got messed up?"

Charles shook his head. "I'll call them when I've got it figured out."

"Can't you ask them to help you out? Housing isn't *that* much."

"Well — " Charles hesitated. It was complicated to explain — his being adopted, wanting his parents to stop *giving* him so much when they could use their money themselves, wanting to be independent — "I'd rather do it myself."

"It's a lot of work."

"It's worth it."

"Yeah, but — hey!" Buddy elbowed him. "There she is!"

Charles squinted. "There who is?"

"Gwendolyn Pierce." Buddy sighed. "Is she beautiful, or what?"

Charles located her, a tall blonde in a lavender sundress, walking with three admiring boys. "Wow."

"Cheryl Tiegs'd commit suicide if she saw Gwendolyn."

"Do you know her name because of matriculation?"

"No, the Face Book."

Charles looked at him blankly.

"You haven't seen the Face Book?"

Charles shook his head.

"Wait a minute." Buddy fished around inside his rucksack, taking out an already dog-eared paperback about the size of a magazine. "You know how Admissions wrote and said you had to send in your picture? They print 'em all in here."

Charles took the book and flipped through it, seeing page after page of small, smiling photographs, with students' names and hometowns under each. "What are the circles for?"

"Oh." Buddy pointed to a green circle around a girl named Felicia Davies. "Green's for the girls I'm maybe going to ask out, and," he pointed to Jacqueline Donaldson, "blue's for the girls I'm *definitely* going to ask out."

Charles flipped ahead to the P's, locating Gwendolyn Pierce easily by the large red circle. "What's red mean?"

"Red means I'd die for her," Buddy said.

They looked at the picture: Gwendolyn, stunning in a dark slinky gown, obviously at the prom.

"Wow," Charles said. "She's the only red circle?"

Buddy nodded. "I've got a couple of pinks, though."

"What's pink mean?"

Buddy grinned. "I'd get real sick."

Charles laughed, and searched through the book until he found Buddy, very tan, teeth very white, holding a surfboard. "Oh, give me a break."

"Hey," Buddy flexed his muscles, "I bet the whole freshman class is putting red circles around that."

"Ha."

"Oh, yeah? Well, let's see *your* picture."

Charles closed the book.

"No way, you're not getting away with that." Buddy grabbed the book and started turning pages. "What's your last name?"

Charles sipped some Coke.

"Don't worry, I'll find it." Buddy kept turning pages. "It has to be — aha!" He studied the photograph; a conservative senior picture, Charles smiling stiffly, wearing a three-piece suit. "That's the best you could do?"

Charles shrugged.

"You need help," Buddy said, then grinned. "Lucky for you, you met me."

Chapter Two

On Sunday afternoon, Charles dressed carefully.

"A jacket even?" Buddy said, watching him.

"It's an interview."

"Yeah, but — you want me to come with you?"

Charles looked at him, sprawled on the top bunk, wearing ancient gray sweatpants, a "California is for lovers" t-shirt, and a pair of mismatched socks. "That's okay."

"Don't recognize style when you see it, Chuck."

"Guess I don't, Bertrand."

Buddy flushed. "Okay, peace." He shook his head. "Never should have told you that."

"Probably not." Charles checked himself in the mirror one last time, then turned. "You think this looks okay?"

"*I'd* hire you."

"You sure?"

"Absolutely." He swung off the bunk. "Give 'em the works, Chas."

"Yeah." Charles smiled responsibly at the mirror. Sincerely. *Dependably*.

"You're going to be late."

"Yeah."

"So go already."

"Yeah." Charles took a deep breath and headed for the door.

Ten Barrington Court *was* within walking distance — once he figured out where he was going. The house was very attractive — large, ranch-style, natural wood stain. The backyard was about half an acre, framed by maple trees. At least, he *thought* they were maple trees. He walked up to the front door, looked at the brass knocker and the doorbell, then chose the bell. A girl about fourteen, wearing two layers of *Flashdance* sweatshirts, opened the door and stared.

"Uh, hi," Charles said. "I'm — "

"A guy," she said, her expression surprised.

"I'm, uh, here about the job?"

"You are?"

"Uh, is this the Pembroke house?"

She nodded and held the door open.

He followed her inside, stopping when he saw a living room full of girls, all of whom stared at him, then nudged companions, giggling. He smiled uneasily and stayed near the door, too self-conscious to go in any further. Weren't there *any* other guys applying for this? The girls were still staring at him and so, being cool, he leaned against the wall, bumping into a table and knocking a lamp off-balance, catching it just before it fell. Bright-red, he put it back on the table and moved to lean against the door instead. The bell rang and he jumped, moving against the stairs, one hand gripping the banister.

The girl who had let him in answered the door, letting in two more girls. That made about a hundred in the living room. Or, at least thirty. A lot, anyway. Too bad Buddy hadn't come.

A girl came over — an attractive girl — and he straightened.

"Is this a frat trick?" she asked.

"No." His voice cracked and he coughed, making it lower. "I mean, no."

"No," she said, and shook her head, going back over to the fireplace.

Embarrassed, he moved to lean against a closet, flinching as one of the folding doors opened and a small space mutant looked at him.

"Did I scare you?" the space mutant asked solemnly.

"N-no." He coughed. You were definitely in bad shape when twelve-year-old space mutants made you nervous.

The mutant lifted a plastic ray gun. "Why have you come here?"

"Uh, well — " Why *had* he come here?

"Speak!"

"I am of the rebel forces," Charles said. "I have come to destroy you and your tyranny."

The mutant laughed a deep and hollow laugh. "You are seven thousand light-years away from Alpha — you have no powers here."

"The power of reason," Charles said, just as solemn. "I need nothing more." Although the power of superior height and weight didn't hurt.

"You dare to arouse my wrath?" the mutant asked.

Charles bent enough to rest an arm on each of the mutant's shoulders. "I dare," he said.

"Really?"

Charles nodded. "Rebels fear nothing but cowardice."

"Yeah?" The mutant lifted his mask, revealing a boy with glasses and reddish-brown hair. "I'm Douglas. Of the Land of Gossamer."

Charles grinned. "I'm from Pennsylvania."

The boy grinned back. "I forgive you that, earthling."

"Likewise."

"We've got Atari — want to play?"

"Well — " Charles glanced across the room as a girl came out of the kitchen and another girl went in. Mr. and Mrs. Pembroke must be doing the interviews in there. "I don't really think I can right now."

"But you like video games?"

Charles nodded. "Broke the record on Space Invaders once."

"Really?" Douglas looked impressed. "I've got an excellent game about Venus. Can we play after?"

"Sure."

Douglas lowered his mask. "I must return to Gossamer now."

"Good luck in hyper-space."

Back to mutant movement, Douglas nodded solemnly, crossing the living room, girls moving uneasily out of the way as he went up the stairs.

The interviews took a long time and Charles

ended up sitting on the stairs, wishing that Douglas would come back. Not that this was an ideal time to be playing video games. The girl who had let him in — Douglas' sister? — had passed a couple of times, generally on her way to the phone.

The front door slammed open and a boy in a grass-stained baseball shirt and jeans ran in, a basketball under one arm.

"Later, Matt!" he yelled out the door, then closed it. He looked at all the girls and headed for the kitchen.

His sister got up, intercepting him. "We're not allowed," she said quietly. "Remember?"

"Yeah, but I need food!"

"So get it later."

"Yeah, but — "

"They're *interviewing*."

"Interviewing?" The boy grinned at her. "You mean, this *isn't* a meeting of the Alexander Morgan Fan Club?"

She stared at him. "Jason, you slime! You read my diary!"

"No, I didn't. I listened in on your phone call with Sarah."

"Jason!"

The kitchen door opened and a man in a tweed jacket looked out. "How about a little quiet out here, guys?" he suggested.

"He listened in when I was on the phone, Dad!"

"Jason, don't listen in when your sister is on the phone," the man said mildly. "And Lila, don't over-react."

"But, Dad!"

"We're almost finished, okay?" He smiled at everyone else in the living room. "We'll be with the rest of you shortly."

"Dad," Jason said, "can't I get —"

"Later, okay?" His father went back into the kitchen.

"Wretched boy," Lila said to Jason.

"Ugly girl," he said and ducked out of the way before she could hit him. He dribbled over to the stairs, stopping when he saw Charles. "How come you're here?"

"To interview with your parents."

"But you're a *guy*."

"So are you."

"They want a girl."

Uneasily, Charles looked at the kitchen. "Did they say that?"

"We always have girls."

"This isn't the first time your parents have advertised?"

"More like the thirtieth."

Charles studied him, harmless enough in untied basketball sneakers, then Lila, sitting on the couch, filing her nails. "You don't *look* too bad."

"It's our brother. He's diseased."

"You mean, the one from the Land of Gossamer."

"Ah," Jason said. "You've met."

"We've met."

Jason snapped a chest pass at him. "Think fast."

Charles caught it automatically and Jason looked pleased.

"Good catch," he said. "Can you do a hook shot?"

Charles snapped the ball back. "Sometimes."

"Can you show me?"

Charles glanced at the kitchen. "Well—"

"Can you show me after?"

"Well—sure."

"How about baseball? Do you like baseball?"

Charles nodded.

"And football?"

Charles nodded.

"Do you play on teams?"

"I did in high school."

"Wow."

"I wasn't that good."

"Bet you were."

"Well, I was okay," he admitted.

"Were you ever captain?"

"Well—yeah. It wasn't that big a deal."

"Wow. You must be really good."

Charles shrugged self-consciously.

"We have a hoop in the driveway. If I go out and practice, can you come out in a while? After you talk to my parents?"

Charles hesitated. If the parents didn't like him, staying around to play with their sons might be kind of inappropriate.

"Please?" Jason asked.

Charles sighed. "Sure."

"Great!" Jason said, and dribbled to the front door.

Charles smiled, watching him go. The kids seemed nice—it would be a lot like having brothers and sisters. He'd always wanted brothers and sisters.

The Pembrokes were down to the last few applicants, and when Mr. Pembroke opened the kitchen door to ask "Who's next?" the remaining girls looked at him.

"Uh, me, sir," he said, standing up.

Mr. Pembroke gestured for him to come in.

Mrs. Pembroke was sitting at the kitchen table and indicated for him to do the same. "You're — ?"

"Charles," he said, sitting down after Mr. Pembroke did.

"Well, I'm Jill and this is my husband, Stan."

Charles nodded at each, very politely.

"I believe you said you were a freshman when we spoke on the phone?"

"Yes, ma'am."

"And what interests you about the job?"

"Well, ma'am, I — " Charles stopped, deciding not to say that he needed the room and board. At least, not that bluntly. "My work-study fell through, and since this would combine both housing and work — " He frowned. Was this coming out right? Probably not.

"Well," Mr. Pembroke said. "Our situation is that my wife has recently gone back to work."

"As an arts critic for the *Meridian*," Mrs. Pembroke explained.

"And as a result, she often gets last minute calls to review shows or gallery openings."

"The first string critic has something of a problem," Mrs. Pembroke said.

"He's a *lush*, Jill," Mr. Pembroke said.

She nodded. "He's a lush, Charles."

Charles grinned, amused by the interplay.

"And," Mr. Pembroke went on, "there's also the time that she has to spend down at the paper, as well as my job and — well, we need someone who will enjoy being here, taking care of things when Jill and I can't."

Mrs. Pembroke nodded. "The boys can be pretty rambunctious. And, well, Lila's at the age."

Charles was going to nod wisely, but wasn't sure what she meant. "Um, which age is that, ma'am?"

"Have you noticed a certain amount of phone activity and giggling?" Mr. Pembroke asked.

Charles nodded.

"*That* age."

Charles grinned. "Got it."

"So," Mrs. Pembroke said, "spending time with little brothers isn't exactly on her list of priorities."

Charles nodded.

"We just want to be sure we find someone who *wants* — "

"Hey, Charles!" Jason called through the back door, from the driveway. "You almost finished?"

His parents looked at Charles, who flushed.

"In a while," he said to Jason. "Okay?"

Jason sighed and dribbled away.

"I, um, I played in high school," Charles said sheepishly. "He wants me to teach him a hook shot."

The Pembrokes exchanged glances.

"Well," Mrs. Pembroke said. "That — "

"Hey!" Douglas said accusingly at the kitchen door. "I thought you were going to play Atari with *me*."

"I, uh — " Charles flushed more. "Can you wait?"

"You promised."

"Yeah, but — "

"No way," Jason said from the back door. "He promised me first!"

"No, I — " He glanced at their parents uneasily. "I'm sorry, I didn't mean to — "

"So, come on," Douglas said. "Let's — "

"No way!" Jason interrupted. "He said he'd—"

Mrs. Pembroke smiled. "Charles, would you like a job?"

Chapter Three

"So you got it," Buddy said.

Charles nodded. "They want me to move in to-morrow."

Buddy whistled. "*Tomorrow?*"

Charles nodded.

"So this is your last night as a free man?"

"No one's making me do this, Buddy — I *want* to." Charles nodded to reassure himself. He *did* want to, especially now that he had met the kids. Yeah. Everything was going to work out fine.

"You sure I can't talk you out of it?" Buddy said.

Charles nodded.

"Think of all the stuff you'll be missing! Parties, girls — "

"Wait a minute," Charles said. "What happens to other people who commute? They hang out at parties, same as anyone."

"If you say so." Buddy shook his head. "Sounds like a lousy deal to me."

"It sounds *great* to me," Charles said.

The next morning, Charles got up so early that

even Martin was still asleep. Everything packed, he moved his suitcase, knapsack, and typewriter near the door, sitting on top of his duffel bag to think.

When he'd called his parents the night before, they had sounded both hurt and proud. Hurt that he felt he couldn't ask them for help, but proud that he was mature enough to handle things on his own. They had, of course, offered to help him out financially, and he had thanked them, but refused. Eighteen was too old to be dependent on them — especially when they had given him so *many* things over the years. Like a home.

Buddy groaned on his bunk and turned over. "You up *already*?" he asked sleepily.

Charles had to grin. "Looks that way."

"You're weird, Charles," Buddy said, and turned over to face the wall. "Very weird."

He *felt* weird these days. In high school, things had been easy — four years of being Mr. Nice Guy. Mr. Sincere. Kind of hard to live up to twenty-four hours a day. When he was out on dates, girls would say, "You're such a nice guy, Charles. It's fun to go out with you." Translation: You're so nice that we know you're not going to try anything. So in spite of the fact that he never had trouble getting a date — and the other guys in his class were envious about that — they weren't exactly real dates either. More than the girls in his school thought, but not nearly as much as the guys thought.

Senior year, he had been on three varsity teams; he'd been captain of the basketball and baseball squads; president of the Student Council; the lead in *Barefoot in the Park*; editor of the yearbook; and third in his class. Everyone expected him to go off and be Joe College somewhere. He'd gotten in everywhere he applied — to which people responded, "That's great, he's such a nice guy" — and he had chosen Crawford College in New Jersey. It was a good school, less than an hour from New York City, but still rural enough to seem like college. And coming from a small town in Pennsylvania, Charles liked the idea of being close to New York.

So how come nothing was working out right? He'd pictured college as being like *Brideshead Revisited* or something — stately, academic, dignified, and still fun. Crawford was *pretty* enough, but not exactly a Serious Place. It would probably be better once classes started, but still. So far, it was like being at camp. And he'd always hated camp. Too frivolous.

"You nervous?"

Charles jumped. "No," he said quickly. "No way."

"Right."

"Look, you don't have to get up. I can just —"

Buddy swung his legs over the side of the bunk and jumped to the floor. No reaction from Martin, asleep on the bottom bunk.

Buddy yawned and, stretching his arms up, grabbed a t-shirt from his bedpost. "Figured I'd come along for the walk." He pulled the shirt over his head. "Think the parents'll mind or anything?" he asked through the material.

Charles frowned. Would they? If he were a parent, *he* would. Nothing like hiring someone who was going to have a bunch of rowdy friends hanging around all the time. "I don't know," he said finally.

Buddy stepped into a pair of jeans, then his sneakers. "Can't expect you to carry all your stuff alone."

Hmmm. That made sense. Charles stood up, tossing Buddy the knapsack. "So, let's go already."

As they left the campus and got closer to Barrington Court, Buddy walked more slowly.

"We're entering into a world more boring than you can imagine," he said in a Rod Serling voice. "A place that knows neither time nor space. A place that knows only — Tupperware."

Charles laughed. "Will you shut up?"

"We are entering — *suburbia*."

Charles pushed him off-balance. "I said, shut up already."

"A world in which only the most — "

"That's it, over there," Charles said, pointing across the street.

"Rich," Buddy said.

"You think?" Charles studied the house, deciding that Buddy was right. He had been too nervous to notice the day before.

"You want me to come up with you, or is it a bad idea?"

"Um, I'm not really sure." Charles swallowed, tightening his grip on his suitcase. This was kind of a big step he was about to take. New responsibilities, rules, demands . . . .

"You nervous?"

"A little, maybe."

Buddy turned, taking a sprinter's ready position. "It's not too late. We can still escape."

Charles grinned. "No, it's okay."

"You're going to leave me all alone in that room with *Martin*?"

"He'll probably be a good influence. Get you to study and stuff."

"Never," Buddy said. He looked down at the duffel bag and typewriter, then at the house. "You're *sure* you want to do this? Like I said, if you needed a loan, I could — "

Charles shook his head. "Thanks, but I really want to do this."

"Okay," Buddy said, accepting that. "Look, I heard pysch 1 is meeting in Harrison. Be out in front at nine-thirty tomorrow and I'll see you there."

Charles started to nod, but stopped. "Wait a minute — psych meets at nine."

"What, you mean you want to show up on *time* or something?" He laughed at Charles' expression. "Responsible and gullible go together, huh?"

"I'm not — "

"Responsible," Buddy nodded. "I know." He stuck out his hand. "Good luck, son. College would've been fun."

"It'll be fun."

"You'd just better get Friday and Saturday nights off."

"Count on it," Charles said. He hoped. At least *some* Friday and Saturday nights.

When Buddy had gone, he carried his bags up the front walk to the door. This time he'd try the knocker maybe. As he lifted his hand to knock, the door opened and he almost fell inside.

Jason grinned up at him. "Hi, Charles."

Charles recovered his balance, and dignity. "Hi, Jason." He glanced down at his bags, not sure if he should bring them in, or —

"Charles!" Mrs. Pembroke said, coming out of the kitchen. "Come in — you live here now."

"Come *in*," Douglas said, moving ominously down the stairs, his face hidden by a Darth Vader mask. "We don't bite," he said and laughed wildly, rubbing his hands in glee.

"*Diseased*," Jason said to Charles.

Mrs. Pembroke picked up the typewriter case and crossed the living room behind the couch. "This is going to be your room, Charles," she said, opening a door. Charles followed with the rest of his things.

The room was nice, with checked wallpaper, the main colors tan and gray. Besides the bed, there was a wooden desk and a bookcase. A bathroom opened off the far side of the room.

"I hope this is all right?" Mrs. Pembroke said.

"Oh, it's fine," Charles said. "Great." He nodded to punctuate that, putting his luggage on the bed.

"Have you had breakfast?"

No. Except that it was eleven, and they had probably already —

"There's plenty in the kitchen," Mrs. Pembroke said. "Why don't you get settled a little and then come in?"

"Yes, ma'am," he said. "Thank you, ma'am."

Jason snickered.

"Take your time, Charles," Mrs. Pembroke said, smiling.

26

"Thank you."

As she left, Jason and Douglas stayed by the bureau, watching him.

"Uh, hi," Charles said.

The boys didn't say anything, Jason grinning, Douglas masked.

"When's school start?"

"Tomorrow," Jason said.

"Me, too." Charles glanced at Douglas. "You, too?"

"In another season," Douglas said solemnly. "In a world that time — "

"Ignored," Jason said.

"*Neglected*," Douglas said.

"What are you two going to do today?" Charles asked, unzipping his suitcase.

They looked at each other, Douglas lifting his mask; then they grinned at him.

"Oh," Charles said.

Breakfast was great — pancakes, sausage, fresh fruit, lots of coffee.

"Don't be shy, Charles," Mrs. Pembroke said. "There's plenty more."

He put down his fork, embarrassed. "I, um — tend to eat a lot, ma'am."

"So do birds," Douglas said, and they all looked at him. "Well, they do. I read it in a book."

"That's why so many birds are *fat*," Jason said.

"That's why Frank Perdue is *rich*," Mrs. Pembroke remarked, pouring herself more coffee.

Charles laughed. So far, being here was pretty good.

Lila came into the kitchen, brushing her hair. "Morning," she said sleepily.

27

"Boy, about *time*," Jason said.

"I wasn't asleep," Lila said defensively.

"She needs lots of beauty rest," Jason explained to Charles.

"Mom!"

"Jason," Mrs. Pembroke said warningly. "Help yourself to some breakfast, Lila."

"No, thanks." She turned to Charles. "I eat like a bird."

He managed to keep himself to a polite grin, although Mrs. Pembroke and the boys laughed.

"A vulture," Jason said.

"You know what vultures eat?" Douglas asked. "Carrion. And then, they — "

"Is that really necessary, Douglas?" Mrs. Pembroke asked.

"It's kind of interesting," he said.

"It's *gross*," Lila said, filling her plate with pancakes and sausage. She looked at Charles. "Okay, a big bird," she said.

"*I* eat like a pterodactyl," he said, helping himself to one more serving.

"Except probably not," Douglas said hesitantly. "Because their diets were mostly — "

They all looked at him.

"Maybe this isn't the time," he said.

"I think you're right," his mother said.

After breakfast, without waiting to be asked, Charles got up to do the dishes.

"Charles," Mrs. Pembroke started, "you don't have to feel as if — "

"It's all right, ma'am." Charles opened the dishwasher, scanning the racks to make sure he knew where to put everything. At home, he had never been very good at it.

"We'll help," Douglas said, Jason nodding.

Mrs. Pembroke stared at them. "You *will*?"

Jason jumped up, carried his plate to the trash can, scraped it, then put it in the sink. Douglas did the same, also carrying his mother's plate.

"Well," Mrs. Pembroke said, standing up with her coffee, "in *that* case." She paused at the door. "Charles, Stan will be home soon and the three of us will sit down and go over your responsibilities, okay?"

"Yes, ma'am," Charles said, rinsing plates.

The boys hung around the sink, watching him, not really helping much.

"Why don't you put away the orange juice and everything?" Charles suggested, and they moved to do so.

"Dad's at work," Jason said, putting the top on the maple syrup.

"On Labor Day?"

"He's in the habit," Douglas said. "Mom made him promise to be home by lunch."

Charles nodded.

"That's why *you're* here," Jason said. "So Mom can do work, too."

Charles nodded. "Do you mind? I mean, do you wish I didn't have to be?"

"You're a guy," Douglas said. "We don't mind a *guy*."

"Good," Charles said. "Because I'm kind of glad to be here."

*   *   *

Later, when Mr. Pembroke got home, he, Mrs. Pembroke, and Charles sat at the dining room table to discuss Things.

"Of course, all of this can be adapted," Mrs. Pembroke said. "Right, Stan?"

"Almost all of it," Mr. Pembroke agreed, putting on his reading glasses to study the papers his wife was holding.

Mrs. Pembroke laughed. "What he means, Charles, is that we want you to feel free to have your friends over, but we would prefer that you didn't have them overnight."

Them meaning *girls*.

"We would downright insist," Mr. Pembroke said pleasantly.

"Oh, absolutely, sir," Charles said, nodding. "It wouldn't be right."

Mr. Pembroke's posture relaxed. "Good."

"What we had in mind, Charles, was your being responsible for getting the children off to school when necessary, being here when they get home — to the degree that your class schedule allows — being 'on call' four or five nights a week, and just generally being helpful when Stan and I have to work. We have a maid, so we don't expect you to do any cleaning, except for heavy work occasionally." Mrs. Pembroke looked up. "How does that sound so far, Charles? Pretty much what we outlined yesterday?"

He nodded.

"You said that you can drive both an automatic and a stick shift?" Mr. Pembroke asked.

"Yes, sir."

"Well, a certain percentage of the job will involve the car — driving the children to lessons, practices, that sort of thing. Maybe picking up groceries — does all of this still sound all right?" Mrs. Pembroke's voice was less certain.

Charles nodded. He seemed to nod a lot lately.

"The important thing is for us to know that when we aren't here, everything is under control. Beyond that, you're free to come and go as you please, eat with us — or earlier, or later — " Mrs. Pembroke's shrug indicated endless possibilities. "We hope, though, that you'll feel like one of the family. That's what we *want*."

So did he. "I'm looking forward to it," Charles said. "Very much."

Chapter Four

Charles spent most of the rest of the day with Douglas and Jason: shooting baskets with Jason, playing Atari with Douglas, watching a *Battlestar Galactica* rerun with both of them. Lila had a couple of friends over, and the three of them kept walking by and giggling, which Charles found both flattering and embarrassing.

"Now what're we going to watch?" Jason asked as the show ended.

"*Nova*," Douglas said, getting up to change the channel.

"No way!" Jason beat him to it, blocking the television. "Charles, can't we watch something better?"

"Well—"

"The Generals are playing. Can't we watch that? Or, on Sportschannel, there's—"

"I'm not watching stupid Sportschannel," Douglas said.

"You all have more than one television, don't you?" Charles asked, figuring that that was a reasonable solution.

"Yeah, but what are *you* going to watch?" Jason asked, both boys looking at him.

"I don't know." He'd never spent much time watching television anyway. "What's on HBO? Or we could turn on MTV."

"*Lila* watches MTV," Jason said, Douglas nodding. "She and her friends dance and everything."

"So, what about HBO?"

Jason turned to HBO where *Not Necessarily the News* was just starting.

"Can we all deal?" Charles asked.

Jason and Douglas nodded.

Charles swung his legs onto the coffee table. "Good."

Mrs. Pembroke made the boys go to bed pretty early to "get ready for their big day."

"Why don't you finish unpacking, Charles?" she suggested. "You have a big day ahead yourself."

"Yes, ma'am," he said. "Thank you."

He was in his room, the door ajar, when Lila knocked.

"Are you busy?" she asked.

He paused with an armload of socks, on his way to the dresser. "No, come on in."

Hesitantly, she stepped into the room, staying near the door. "You look busy."

Charles dumped the socks into the second drawer, closed it, and sat on top of his desk. "I'm not."

"But you were."

He shook his head.

"Oh." She looked at the door, shifting her weight from one leg to the other. "I guess you're going to hang out with Jason and Douglas mostly, right? I mean, because they're boys and stuff."

Charles shrugged. "Not necessarily."

"I don't play sports or those dumb science games or anything."

"That's not all I do either," Charles said.

"Do you have brothers and sisters and stuff at home?"

"No. I always wanted some."

"Sisters, too?"

He nodded.

"That's good. I figured maybe you didn't." She shifted her weight again. "I guess Mom and Dad think I'm not old enough to take care of stuff."

"I think Mom and Dad don't want to cramp your style," Charles said. "Besides, they need someone who can drive."

"Yeah, I guess so." She looked up, a little grin starting. "Do you like to drive?"

"Sure."

"Like to malls and stuff? After school?"

Charles also grinned. "Sure. Malls are great."

Completely unpacked, he was lying on his new bed, reading the new Vonnegut book, when someone knocked on the door.

"Um, hello?" he said, sitting up. "I mean, come in."

Mr. Pembroke opened the door. "Just wanted to make sure that everything was okay."

Charles stood up, checking to see if his shirt was buttoned. "Yes, sir. Thank you."

"Good."

Charles nodded, expecting him to leave, but he didn't.

"Good book," Mr. Pembroke said, indicating the paperback.

"Um, yes, sir. So far." Self-conscious, Charles put it on the table next to his bed. "My, uh, my English teacher recommended it."

"Ah," Mr. Pembroke said, nodding.

Charles nodded back.

"I was able to speak to your principal last night. Your basketball coach, too."

Charles nodded. He had given them, as well as a couple of teachers, as references.

"They said you were an excellent student. Dependable, responsible — everything Jill and I suspected during the interview."

"Well," Charles said, embarrassed.

"And, in a way, I feel better that you're male. It seems — safer."

How was he supposed to respond to *that*?

"How do you think your courses are going to be?"

"I don't know, sir." Were classes going to fall into the same pattern of not quite being what he'd imagined? "Challenging, I guess."

"I hope that this" — Mr. Pembroke's gesture indicated the house in general — "doesn't interfere too much."

"No, sir. I'm sure it won't."

"Well." Mr. Pembroke folded his arms. "I'm glad we had this talk."

"Yes, sir."

"No need to call me 'sir,' Charles."

"No, Mr. Pembroke. I mean, I won't."

"Good. Let us know if you need anything."

Charles nodded.

*　　*　　*

Breakfast was hectic, all of them running a little late, all of them having to be somewhere at the same time.

"Charles," Mrs. Pembroke said, skimming the article she was handing in one last time, "I have to cover an opening at the gallery this afternoon. If I leave you a list and some money, would you mind picking up some groceries after class?"

Charles nodded. "No problem, Mrs. Pembroke."

"Can I come, too?" Jason asked, shiny clean in a new blue shirt, darker crewneck, and tan chinos.

"Me, too?" Douglas asked, also very clean in a white shirt, his *Return of the Jedi* belt, and blue corduroys.

"I'll wait for you guys to get home before I go." Charles checked his watch, then glanced around the kitchen. No one else looked ready to leave yet, and it wouldn't be right for him to be the first one to go, but —

"Are you going to be late for class?" Mrs. Pembroke asked.

"Um, possibly." He checked his watch again. Almost definitely.

"Then you'd better go."

"I thought he was going to take all of us to school," Lila said from the phone where she was talking to one of her friends about what both of them were wearing and whether or not they should change.

Charles looked at her, alarmed. The Pembrokes hadn't said anything about that. By the time he got the three of them to school, wherever the schools were, it would be so late that —

"She's kidding," Mrs. Pembroke assured him. "They all walk to school."

"Fine neighborhood to bring up children," Mr. Pembroke said, behind the morning edition of the *Times*.

"A *fine* neighborhood," Jason said and his father lowered the newspaper enough to frown at him.

"Charles, go," Mrs. Pembroke said. "Don't be late the first day."

Charles nodded. "Thank you." He stood up, taking his notebook — three new spirals, one for each of the classes he was going to have today — off the counter. "I guess I'll see all of you later."

"Beware of alpha rays, young warrior," Douglas said in a deep voice.

Charles grinned. "You, too."

He was a little more casual today — his shirt collar open, his tie loosely knotted, then tucked into his shirt — but he still felt as if now that he was in college it was time to put in a little effort. Be mature.

When he got to the campus, Buddy was waiting on the steps of the psychology building.

"Sorry I'm late," Charles said, out of breath. "They were all going to school."

"You have to take them?"

"No. Just have breakfast with the family."

"The *family*." Buddy shook his head. "Weird."

"Where is everyone?" The campus seemed strangely empty, the quad quiet and green.

"Class." Buddy yawned. "Or asleep. Sure wish I was."

"Are we really late?"

"Five, ten minutes." Buddy stood, stretching. "Come on, we meet in the auditorium in here."

"*Auditorium?*"

"It's psych 1, what do you expect?"

"Well, the catalog said the student/teacher ratio was — "

"When you're a senior, maybe. Not for intro classes."

"How *big* an auditorium?" Charles asked, following him.

"Big enough for three hundred."

"Three *hundred*? What happens if you want to ask a question?"

Buddy shrugged. "I guess you do that in those section meetings we're supposed to have on Fridays."

"But those are run by teaching assistants. What happens if you want to talk to the professor?"

Buddy stuck out his hand, very solemn. "Welcome to college, son."

The auditorium was large and crowded, with old blue seats and a proscenium stage with a lab table and a professor behind a podium, his name printed across the blackboard in huge letters that were still hard to read from the back.

They found seats on the far right aisle, maybe thirty rows back, and sat down. Charles lifted the little fold-up desk from the right side of his chair and opened his notebook.

"It's the first day," Buddy said. "You don't have to take *notes*."

"Maybe he's saying something important."

"On the first day?"

Charles nudged him to be quiet, trying to listen.

"So, how's it going with the family?"

"Buddy!"

Buddy sighed deeply. "I'm telling you, Charles, it's the first day. He isn't saying anything important."

"He's telling us what books we have to buy."

"So what? We'll find two girls after class and ask them. It's a great way to start a conversation."

"You must read *Seventeen* faithfully," Charles said, eyes on the professor.

Buddy flushed. "Okay, okay, I'll be quiet."

"Good." Charles leaned forward, hoping that it would be easier to hear that way. Not much difference.

"I don't read *Seventeen*," Buddy said.

Charles nodded, listening.

"I mean, my sister has a subscription, and if I was bringing in the mail, I might *look* at it for a minute, but that doesn't mean that I — "

"Buddy, will you be quiet already?"

"Just wanted to be sure that was clear."

Charles nodded.

"So, okay, then." Buddy sat back and folded his arms, looking around the auditorium.

Relieved, Charles gave his full attention to the professor, who was now outlining the way they would all be graded — a midterm, a final, performance in section. . . .

"Hey!" Buddy elbowed him. "Check it out!"

Charles sighed. "What?"

"Middle section, twelfth row, third seat in."

Charles looked, seeing long, blonde hair, tanned shoulders, sundress straps. Gwendolyn Pierce.

"I know who *I'm* asking about the books," Buddy said.

"Buddy, she's already sitting with about eight guys — you don't have a chance."

"*Buddy* Lembeck, not have a chance? You're kidding, right?"

"*Bertrand* Lembeck would probably do better."

"Ha," Buddy said.

When class was over, which the professor indicated by glancing at his watch, stepping away from the lectern and nodding once, Gwendolyn Pierce left, surrounded by freshmen males.

"Sublime," Buddy said, watching her. "Just plain sublime."

"For once," Charles said, also watching, "I agree with you."

They hung out on the grass in front of the Student Center for a while, watching the huge crowd as classes changed, and then the relative emptiness of the campus at five after ten. It stayed that way until ten of eleven when they separated to go to their eleven-o'clock classes. Buddy was taking Introduction to the American Political System, a course his brother had described as a "major gut." Charles walked to one of the other social science buildings for his Introductory Macro and Microeconomics course, the first requirement for business majors. The course had a reputation for being pretty tough — so many people wanted to major in economics that the department used the introductory course to weed out as many people as possible.

It was held in another auditorium, this one big enough for about one hundred and fifty students, and most of the seats were taken. The atmosphere here was quite different from his psychology class — quiet, tense, academic. He had heard that generally a third of the class dropped the course after receiving their midterm grades.

Even today, that was obvious. After a short introduction, the professor went right into her first lecture, everyone taking quick, nervous notes. Hearing pens and pencils moving furiously on nearby notebook pages, Charles relaxed. *This* was more like it. Difficult, challenging, intense — College. He picked up his own pen and started writing.

Chapter Five

At twelve, Charles met Buddy in one of the dining halls for lunch, showing his student ID and paying a reduced guest rate for lunch. Not exactly inexpensive, but as long as it was for only one meal a day, he could afford it.

"This is great," Buddy said, piling food on his tray. "I love this."

Charles looked at all of the desserts on the tray. "I bet your mother thinks you're eating nutritious meals."

"I'll get plenty of nutrition at Thanksgiving." Buddy reached back over two people's trays to take an apple. "There. That better?"

"Oh, yeah."

"So," Buddy said when they were sitting down, speaking more loudly than usual to be heard over the noise of several hundred other students, "economics as hard as they say?"

Charles nodded, taking a huge bite of his hamburger. "Definitely." He stopped chewing. "This food is really terrible."

"Yeah." Buddy ate four french fries at once. "But there's lots of it."

"Some jock *you* are."

Buddy grinned, flexing his muscles as he lifted one of his three brownies. "Hey, want to hear an excellent joke about Martin?"

Charles shrugged. "Sure."

"How many pre-meds does it take to change a light bulb?"

"No idea."

"Two," Buddy said. "One to screw in the bulb, and the other to knock the chair out from underneath him."

Charles laughed, picturing skinny, bespectacled Martin kicking someone's chair.

"Pretty good, huh?" Buddy said. "Some guy on my hall told it to me."

"Not bad," Charles agreed.

"He told me this other one about —" Buddy stopped, looking at something across the cafeteria. "Uh, look," he said. "Guess I forgot to tell you something."

Charles tilted his head. "What?"

"Hi, Buddy," a girl said, stopping at their table, holding a tray with a glass of Tab, a large salad from the salad bar, and some cake. "Sorry we're late." She smiled at Charles. "Hi. You must be Charles."

"Uh, hi," Charles said, automatically standing up. He shot a glance at Buddy, who smiled innocently.

"Here." Buddy moved his knapsack off one chair, Charles' books off another. "We saved you two seats."

"*We*," Charles said quietly.

"Yeah," Buddy said, also quiet. "Should have mentioned it, I guess."

Charles nodded.

"Marcy, Beth, this is my friend Charles."

The girls smiled and Charles, for lack of another reaction, smiled back.

"Please," he said to the girl closest to him — Marcy? — holding out a chair. "Sit down."

"How *charming*," she said, and sat down.

"Uh, yeah." Buddy jumped up to hold Beth's chair, but she was already sitting. "Yeah," he said uncertainly, and pushed the chair in a little.

"Is it true that you're working your way through school?" Beth was asking Charles.

"Well —" Charles hesitated. *Kind of.* "Uh, to a degree, yes," he said, his voice a little deeper. "But I have a scholarship."

"Academic?" Marcy asked.

"Well — yeah," Charles said, not sure if that would make him gain or lose points.

"Buddy, you were right," Marcy said. "He *is* great."

"And *cute*," Beth said.

Gain. Self-consciously, Charles picked up his hamburger.

"Plays sports, too," Buddy said, and flexed his muscles. "We both do."

"What do you play?" Marcy asked.

"Oh, just about everything. Right, Charles?"

Charles nodded. "Hockey, lacrosse, bocce — you name it."

The girls were appropriately impressed —

which wasn't much, but enough for Buddy to talk everyone into a double date for Friday before they all had to go to one-o'clock classes.

"So, can we operate or what?" Buddy asked as they left the dining hall to go to their Freshman Writing class. "What a team!"

"Not bad," Charles conceded.

"And I had 'em both circled in the Face Book, too!" He slung his arm around Charles' shoulders. "I'm telling you, Charles, we're on our way."

"On our way to being *late*," Charles said.

Buddy squinted up at the clock on the tower of the administration building. "That, too."

After English class — during which they were given a 1,500-word paper assignment about "My High School," due Thursday, plus some reading — Charles went to the bookstore with Buddy to pick up their books.

It was very crowded, upperclassmen elbowing hesitant freshmen out of the way in the narrow rows between shelves.

"Hey!" Charles said, opening the textbook for their psychology class. "This is thirty dollars!"

"Your economics book is probably even more expensive," Buddy guessed. "More specialized and all. My brother says you can pick up second-hand ones sometimes after the first drop date."

"That's three weeks into the semester!"

Buddy shrugged. "You can always catch up on the reading."

"Yeah, but if you get that far behind, you probably have to drop the class anyway."

Buddy shrugged again.

"My books will cost over a hundred dollars!"

"So will mine," Buddy said. "Guess that means I'd better read them, huh?"

"I guess so." Charles closed his eyes when he saw the price inside his economics book: thirty-five dollars. Plus the psychology book: sixty-five dollars, and he hadn't even looked for the books he would need in his other two courses. Thank God he had a place to live.

After waiting in line long enough to get nervous — the boys would be getting home from school soon — Charles paid one-hundred-forty dollars for his new books, which fit into one bag without too much trouble. One-hundred-forty dollars worth of books should have taken up at least three bags. It had taken *him* at least sixty hours of work over the summer. Pretty depressing.

"Some guys are getting up a game of Ultimate Frisbee," Buddy said as they left the bookstore. "You into it?"

Yes. "I can't," Charles said. "The boys will be home from school in a while."

"So there's no way?"

Charles shook his head.

"Well, maybe next time. When's your first class tomorrow?"

"I have French at ten. Then, my economics section in the afternoon."

"See you outside the dining hall at noon?"

Charles nodded. "Have a good game."

"Yeah," Buddy said, looking guilty. "Tell you

what — at lunch tomorrow, we'll get some dates for Saturday night."

"What about Marcy and Beth? They seem pretty nice."

"Go out with them *twice* in a row? You're kidding, right?"

"What if we like them?"

"They're *girls*," Buddy said. "Of course we'll like them."

Charles stared at him. "That's it?"

"Yeah. We're not going to *marry* them."

"Yeah, but —" Charles checked his watch. "You're weird, Buddy."

"And you're late."

"Yeah." Charles hefted his bag of new books. Too heavy to run, but he could walk fast. "See you tomorrow."

"With *women*," Buddy promised.

Charles made it to the Pembrokes' house right before Jason did. He was already sitting at the kitchen table with a Coke when Jason came slamming in, dumping his books on the table.

"Hi, Charles," he said cheerfully, opening the refrigerator. "What's to eat?"

"How was school?" Charles asked, feeling ridiculously like someone's mother.

"Boring." Jason closed the door, holding a banana and two fudge brownies. Charles leaned forward to take one of the brownies for himself. "When are we going shopping?"

"As soon as Douglas gets home."

"Bet he's staying after to make friends with his

teachers," Jason said with his mouth full. He swallowed. "He *likes* teachers."

"Some teachers are nice."

"Yeah, well, I've never met one," Jason said. "My teacher is so mean. . . ." He paused, waiting.

Charles smiled pleasantly, going to the refrigerator to take out the brownie pan.

"*So* mean," Jason said.

Charles helped himself to three.

"So mean," Jason said less confidently.

Charles relented. "How mean was she?"

Jason beamed. "So mean that she hit ten kids in the class. With a *yardstick*."

"Jason, she can't do that — corporal punishment is against the law."

"Yeah, but she's a *sergeant*," Jason said, and laughed. "Got you, Charles!"

Charles grinned sheepishly.

The back door opened and Douglas came in, less exuberant than Jason had been.

"Hi. How was school?" Charles asked.

Douglas sat down. "Fine."

"Anything interesting happen?"

"No."

"Meet any new kids?"

"Just a bunch of stupid earthlings." Douglas sighed and took a brownie.

"And you couldn't get anyone to beam you up?" Charles guessed, figuring that Douglas was the kind of student who made other people nervous because he was a "brain."

"Not until the bell rang." Douglas took another brownie.

48

"The first day is always the worst."

"You think so?"

"I *know* so," Charles said. It sounded right, anyway. "Come on, let's motivate out of here."

"That means 'get groceries,'" Douglas said to Jason, as though he were a member of a very primitive species.

"I know what he means," Jason said, offended. "I'm not stupid."

"Just missing a few brain waves."

"I am not! You're the one who —"

"Come on, guys," Charles said. "Let's get out of here." He took the list, the money, and the car keys Mrs. Pembroke had left, and walked outside, waiting for Jason and Douglas to come out before locking the door.

Lila was just coming up the driveway, wearing a different outfit than the one Charles had seen that morning — fashionable gray-striped pants, cut to the ankle, a gauzy white blouse, large pink hoop earrings, and pink sneakers. "Where are you guys going?"

"Cruising for chicks," Jason said, beating Douglas to the front seat.

Au pairs should promote goodwill among siblings. "Jason," Charles said, making his voice stern.

"Sorry." He turned to Lila. "Cruising for *babes*."

Lila laughed. "In a station wagon?"

"Buying groceries," Charles said. "Want to come?"

"With *them*?" she asked, and thought about

that for a minute. "The mall?" she asked, sounding more interested.

"Sure. Get in."

Inside the store, Charles scanned the list. A long list. "Well." He lowered it and pulled a shopping cart from the end of the row just past the door. "So."

The boys and Lila looked at him, and he looked around at the vegetable department.

"If we split up," he said, "it'll go faster."

"Into teams!" Jason said. "We can race!"

"I *don't* race," Douglas said.

Lila nodded. "For once, I agree with you, spaceman."

"So we won't race," Charles said diplomatically, and studied his list. "Lila, why don't you get some apples and bananas. Douglas, you get a bag of onions and a bag of potatoes. Jason, you get some broccoli and —"

"Gross." Jason shook his head. "No way."

"What do you mean?"

"Mom might make me *eat* it, but no way am I picking it out."

"Okay, okay," Charles said. "Do you like potatoes and onions?"

"When they're french fried."

"Then you get the potatoes and onions, and Douglas, *you* get the broccoli and some asparagus."

Jason clutched his throat, pretending to gag.

"And I," Charles ignored him, "will get some salad stuff."

When they had all returned, Charles looked at the basket.

"Good," he said. "Next section."

"Can I push the cart?" Jason asked.

"Sure." Charles surrendered the handle, and Jason shoved the cart forward, making it career on two wheels. "Uh, not too fast, Jason."

"Man was originally herbivorous, you know," Douglas said conversationally.

"He lived on *herbs*?" Jason said. "Gross."

"A study of the molars makes it obvious." He looked at Charles. "Isn't that right?"

"Well — yeah," Charles said. Not that he would ever turn down a Big Mac if someone offered it.

"The best football player in the world would probably be better if he concentrated on carbohydrates and vegetable proteins," Douglas went on.

"They need *steak*," Jason said. "For muscle."

"Except they don't. Like, eating beans and rice together makes a complete protein and the system can absorb — "

"I don't *believe* this conversation," Lila said, sounding wounded.

"It's true," Douglas said.

"It's *boring*. It's also making me — " She stopped. "Oh no!"

Charles jumped, expecting serious trouble. "What?"

"It's Valerie Hollings. With her mother."

Charles looked ahead, seeing a tall, blonde woman with a smaller blonde girl, both of them very attractive and elegant. "Yeah," he said. "So?"

"You don't understand, Charles." Lila stayed behind him, hiding. "She's perfect! She's going out with a *tenth* grader!"

51

"Wow," Charles said.

"I can't let her see me with *them*." She pointed at Jason and Douglas who were wrestling over a loaf of cracked wheat bread that Douglas was trying to put into the cart. "I'll never live it down."

"Hello, Lila," Valerie said, passing, managing to look down her nose even though she was shorter.

"Hi," Lila muttered, staring at the shelves of bread.

"Are those your brothers?"

Assuming that she meant Jason and Douglas, Lila was going to shake her head, but saw that Valerie was including Charles and looking very impressed.

"Why, yes," she said. "They are."

Valerie's eyes widened. "*He's* your brother?" she asked.

Lila nodded. "Sure is."

"How old is he?"

"*Very* old," Lila said in an "out of your league" voice.

"Wow." Valerie saw that her mother had gone ahead and moved to catch up with her. "Uh, see you in school tomorrow."

"Really? I mean, yeah," Lila said. When Valerie was out of earshot, she turned to Charles. "Thanks."

Charles grinned wryly. "Don't mention it."

Chapter Six

"Everyone have a nice day today?" Mr. Pembroke asked at the dinner table.

Lila sighed, Douglas shrugged, and Jason nodded.

"Good, good," Mr. Pembroke said absentmindedly. "Glad to hear it. Good day, Charles?"

"Yes, sir. It was fine."

Mr. Pembroke nodded. "Good. Jill?"

"Fine, dear," she said. "Although the exhibit wasn't quite what I had hoped. How was your day?"

"Fairly productive, I think. Douglas, eat your chicken — your mother worked very hard to make it."

"No, I didn't, Stan," Mrs. Pembroke said. "I just —"

"Eat your chicken, Douglas."

Douglas picked up his knife, cutting the chicken into smaller pieces.

Mr. Pembroke nodded, satisfied, and when he looked away, Douglas put the knife down, setting his fork next to it.

"Do you have a lot of course work tonight, Charles?" Mrs. Pembroke asked.

Two chapters in psychology, three long chapters for economics, a fifteen-hundred-word essay, and six chapters due in English. "Some, ma'am."

"Well, you can take most of the evening to — "

The phone rang.

"I've got it!" Lila said and ran across the room. "Hello? . . . Oh." She put her hand over the receiver. "Mom, it's for you. Sounds like Mr. Wilson."

Mrs. Pembroke sighed and looked at her husband, who also sighed.

"That means Fletcher's drunk again and she has to cover something last-minute," Jason explained to Charles.

"Jason, don't talk about Mr. Fletcher that way," Mr. Pembroke said. "It's not respectful."

"Yeah, but it's true."

"That's not the point."

"Okay." Jason turned to Charles. "*Mr.* Fletcher."

Charles grinned.

Mrs. Pembroke finished talking on the phone and hung up, returning to the table. "Well, Fletcher's drunk again," she said, picking up her fork.

"Jill!" Mr. Pembroke exclaimed.

"Mr. Wilson wants to know if we can get into the city in time to review an off-Broadway show," Mrs. Pembroke said.

Mr. Pembroke looked at his watch.

"Eight-thirty curtain," she added.

"I suppose so," Mr. Pembroke said grumpily. "If we leave now."

"That's what I said." She looked at Charles. "I'm sorry. Is this going to be a problem for you?"

"Not at all," Charles assured her.

"Will you be able to finish your work?"

"Yes, ma'am. No problem." He hoped.

"Well, okay then." She looked at Mr. Pembroke. "Okay, Stan?"

He put his napkin on the table. "Just tell me that it isn't experimental."

"Hmmm." Mrs. Pembroke bit her lip. "Does it have to be true?"

Mr. Pembroke sighed. "That's what I figured."

After the Pembrokes left, Charles got the boys to clear the table, and Lila to load the dishwasher while he washed the pans.

"Who's going to set the table for breakfast?" he asked cheerfully.

Three blank expressions looked back at him.

"If each of you sets two places, it'll be done."

"What about the cereal?" Jason asked.

"*I'll* do the cereal," Charles said. "Okay?"

They set the table.

"Now," Charles said when they were finished, feeling pretty confident of his authority. "We're all going to do homework, right?"

"Ha," Lila said, and went to the telephone.

"Mr. T's on," Jason said, heading for the den.

Charles looked at Douglas.

"I don't have any," Douglas said.

"Not even a little?"

Douglas shook his head.

"Do you watch Mr. T?"

Douglas winced, and shook his head.

"Does that mean I have to play Atari?"

"You don't *have* to," Douglas said.

"How about we play for a while, and then I work for a while?"

Douglas nodded. "I'll go set it up in the living room."

Charles fixed two glasses of Coke, took some of the brownies that were left, and went out into the living room. Douglas was already playing, wearing his astronaut's helmet.

"Can you see with that thing on?" Charles asked, sitting next to him on the couch.

"They're designed for that, Charles."

"Hmmm." Charles thought about that. "You're probably right."

Douglas nodded, firing missiles at invading spaceships, protecting his planet.

"So, tell me what happened at school today," Charles said, when it was time to take his turn.

Douglas shrugged.

"You weren't too happy when you got home today." Looking over to see Douglas' reaction, Charles missed some spaceships, which got past to attack his planet.

"You just lost your planet," Douglas said.

"Well, it's a pretty big universe." Charles let him take over. "So tell me about school."

"I have to concentrate."

"Not *that* hard."

Douglas kept playing.

"Is your teacher okay?"

56

Douglas shrugged affirmatively, hitting one of the spaceships late as a result.

"What about the kids?"

Douglas' shrug was more hesitant, and a spaceship got by, blowing away half of the planet.

"What's wrong with them?"

"Nothing." Douglas shot many more missiles than he needed, wiping out the fresh battalion of spaceships.

"How come you said they were stupid earthlings?"

Douglas didn't answer; his hand relaxed on the joystick, letting his planet be annihilated.

"Douglas?"

"Well, they *are* stupid," he said.

"Why?"

"They just are!"

"Why?" Charles asked, more gently, and when Douglas didn't answer, leaned forward to turn off the game. "Come on, you can tell me about it."

"Because they fool around all the time."

"You fool around sometimes."

"Not at *school*," Douglas said. He scowled down at the fists in his lap. "And if you *don't* fool around, they don't like you."

Charles nodded.

"I don't want to fool around. I want to *learn* stuff."

Charles nodded.

"Like when they go outside to play something stupid like kickball. Why should I have to play some stupid game when I'd rather read? But if I don't go out and play the stupid game, everyone thinks I'm weird." Douglas slouched down, lowering the visor of his astronaut helmet. "They think I'm weird, anyway," he muttered.

"Because you get good grades?"

"I guess."

"Aren't there other people in your class who get good grades?"

"*Girls.*"

"Ah," Charles said. "I see." He moved his hand through his hair, thinking. "I thought you said that you used to play Dungeons and Dragons with some guys."

"Jake and Jarret moved — they were twins," he explained, seeing Charles' expression, "and Norman's at the junior high now."

"So you're still friends, but he's not at your school anymore."

Douglas nodded.

"You could still play D and D."

"With only two guys?"

Charles was about to say that he had played on and off for a couple of years, but decided that the point was for Douglas to make more friends his own age. "Ask around. There're bound to be people in your class who'd be interested."

"What if there aren't any?"

"Then — " Charles stopped. What if there weren't? "Out of your whole grade? There are bound to be a couple."

"My grade? I thought you said my *class.*"

"Class meaning grade," Charles said smoothly, and picked up a brownie.

"I have to talk to my whole grade?"

"No. Just ask around. Don't worry, it's easier than it sounds."

"Good," Douglas said. "Because it sounds *hard*."

"It really isn't. Like during science, look around and see who's listening. That way, you find people who have something in common with you."

"I guess." Douglas shook his head at the brownie Charles offered. "I bet *you* were always popular."

"No, not really." Charles thought back, remembering being very serious and studious until he was in the eighth grade or so. He had always behaved very well in class, brought home excellent grades, didn't cause trouble, so that his parents would be pleased with him. Although he couldn't remember ever living anywhere else, being adopted had always made him feel as if he ought to behave, just in case his parents changed their minds and sent him back. Intellectually, he'd known — even then — that that would never happen, but he couldn't help thinking about it. Worrying. "For a long time, I was the class brain."

"Yeah?" Douglas took off his helmet, interested. "What happened?"

"I don't know. Relaxed a little, I guess. Decided to stop trying to be what I thought I *should* be, and just be myself." Actually, he was still working on it. "I mean, I kept studying, but I did other things, too."

"*Sports*," Douglas said.

"I played some sports," Charles agreed. "But I liked them. There's no reason to do something you don't like. You could always join the band, or the school newspaper, or any one of a number of things." What a parent expression. "You know what the big thing at Crawford is? 'Diversity.' That's practically all the catalog talks about. That's the *point* of going to school — getting a lot of different people together and trying to work with one another." Charles nodded to emphasize that.

"Oh," Douglas said, his voice somewhere between doubt and sarcasm. "To the 'common goal'?"

"The primary goal," Charles agreed solemnly. "Target: knowledge."

Douglas laughed.

"Route: unknown."

Douglas laughed again. "Destination: a world where people work and look as one."

"A world never explored, light-years beyond the nearest — "

"Weird," Lila said on her way through the room to the kitchen. "Very, very weird."

It was hard to juggle school *and* his responsibilities at the Pembrokes, but after the first week or so, Charles had a pretty good routine going. Get up, study a little before breakfast, see everyone off, go to classes, study in the library for an hour or two — or whenever he wasn't hanging out with Buddy — come back home, drive the kids places or play with them, have dinner, study after the kids went to bed. So far, it seemed to be working pretty well. Three days a week, he even had time after his last class to do some running or play basketball in the gym at school. Buddy always wanted to work out on the Nautilus machines, but Charles could generally talk him out of it.

Wednesday morning, there was a knock on the door as he was getting dressed.

"Charles?" Mrs. Pembroke asked.

Swiftly, he buttoned his shirt, then opened the door. "Good morning."

She smiled. "Good morning. I wanted to ask if you would mind fixing breakfast this morning and seeing everyone off. Stan's car won't start, and I'm going to take him in early so I won't be late myself."

His first time cooking since he'd moved in. "No problem, Mrs. Pembroke."

When he got to the kitchen, it was barely eight-fifteen, so he decided to go all out and fix pancakes and bacon. The kids would like that.

"What's for breakfast?" Jason asked, coming in as Charles was mixing the pancake batter.

"All kinds of good stuff," Charles said. "Pour everyone some orange juice, okay?"

Automatically, Jason went to the refrigerator and took out the orange juice carton. "Do you know how to cook?"

"Sure." Charles started melting butter in the large skillet. "What do you think?"

"Oh, wow," Lila said from the door. "I thought Mom was kidding."

Charles opened the bacon package. "She wasn't."

Lila came over to examine what he was doing, then leaned toward him. "Which do you think is better?"

"What?"

"The eyeshadow." She closed one eye, then the other. "Which do you like better?"

"He likes the clean, natural look," Douglas said, ray-gunning his way into the room.

"Well, I don't know," Charles said. "The blue's okay."

"Just 'okay'?" Lila asked.

"I mean, it's very nice."

"Not sultry?"

"Well —"

"Of course," Lila said quickly, "this is daytime wear."

"Well, then." Charles made a production out of studying her eyes again, and then said, "Definitely the blue."

"What's wrong with the purple?"

"A little overstated," Charles said, and went back to his cooking.

Lila frowned and sat down at the table, opening her eye makeup case and comparing her eyes in the mirror.

Charles put four pieces of bacon in the other frying pan and set the heat at medium, adjusting the gas until the flame seemed just right. Then he spooned some batter onto the large skillet, forming four pancakes. Then, he stepped away, spatula in one hand, spoon in the other, and folded his arms to watch what happened.

"I don't think you know how to cook," Lila said doubtfully.

"Hey," Charles said, turning the bacon, "I worked at McDonald's."

"Yeah, but this is flame-broiled!" Jason said and laughed.

"What it is," Douglas said, "is dead pig."

Lila shuddered. "Don't be gross."

"And sodium nitrates. You know what sodium nitrates do to you?"

"Charles, make him shut up."

"Douglas, shut up," Charles said without turning.

"First" — Douglas folded his hands — "they move through your esophagus down to your stomach where digestive juices —"

Lila put down her makeup sponge. "Douglas, if you don't shut up, I'll scream."

"— and since there aren't any nutrients, the nitrates go into your bloodstream and —"

"Douglas!"

"And the large intestine starts —"

Lila screamed.

"Don't do that!" Charles said, dropping the spatula.

Jason grinned at him. "Dad'd throw fits if he knew you were yelling at us."

"I wasn't," Charles said quickly. "I mean, I didn't. I mean — gosh."

"Hey, Charles!" Douglas pointed.

"In a minute, okay?" Charles said. "Jason, look, I wasn't —" He smelled smoke and turned to see the bacon burning. "Oh —" *Don't swear, Mr. Pembroke would throw a fit* — "Rats."

Lila and her brothers laughed.

"Ratfink," Charles said, relaxing into a smile. He turned off the heat under the bacon, then looked at the now smoking pancakes. "Well — shoot." He turned off the heat, then put down his spatula. "How about some Cheerios, guys?"

Chapter Seven

"So, when am I going to see this place?" Buddy asked. "You've been living there over three weeks and you haven't even asked your best pal over."

"That's true," Charles said, going over the passage he had to translate for French class.

"Are you not allowed or something?"

"Well, I guess I am," Charles said uncertainly. So far, he hadn't felt quite *that* at home.

"So, let's go this afternoon."

"I guess."

"Look," Buddy said, "I'll even bring some books, pretend we're going to study — they'll love that."

"I *do* have to study," Charles said. "We've got that paper due on Monday, and — "

"So we'll work on our papers," Buddy said. "Come on, Charles, it's like you're in solitary confinement over there."

"I told Lila I'd drive her over to the mall."

"Then, we'll drive her over to the mall."

"And I told Jason —"

"We'll do that, too. What time do you get out of class?"

"Two."

"Okay, I'll meet you in front of Fairweather, and —"

"Hi, Charles; hi, Buddy," a girl from their English class said, passing their table.

"Hi," Charles said.

"Hi." Buddy lowered his voice. "Catch you later, Charles." He jumped up, going after the girl. "Hey, Janice, wait up!"

Charles laughed, watching him go. What a wolf.

After classes, as they walked to the Pembrokes, Buddy went into his Rod Serling-Suburbia routine.

"Come on," Charles said. "Enough already."

"Okay, okay." Buddy shifted his knapsack to his other shoulder. "Hey, did I tell you?"

"Tell me what?"

"Got Janice to go with me to the DTD party on Saturday."

"Fast work."

Buddy hung his head modestly. "What can I say?" He straightened up. "Anyway, now all we have to do is get a date for you."

Charles shook his head. "I can't go. Mr. and Mrs. Pembroke are going out and I said I'd stay with the kids."

"Again?"

"It's my job, Buddy."

"Yeah, but you keep missing out on great parties."

"There'll be other parties." Charles took the Pembrokes' mail out of the box.

"I guess so." Buddy shook his head. "I still think it's a lousy deal."

Charles just grinned, bending to pick up one of the empty trash cans near the curb, taking another with his left hand. "Give me a hand with these, will you?"

"I don't even get into the house yet and I'm already a slave?" Buddy carried the other two cans, depositing them next to Charles'. He looked at Charles, going through the mail, separating it. "You actually enjoy this, don't you?"

Charles shrugged. "I like doing my share." He opened one of the envelopes, reading the letter as he unlocked the door to let them inside.

"Who's it from?" Buddy asked, following him.

"My parents." He took a twenty-dollar bill out of the envelope and grinned sheepishly.

"Hey, what's that for?"

"It says," Charles scanned the letter, "for me to 'go buy a pizza.'" He shook his head. "They keep doing this."

"They're your parents, what do you expect?"

Charles just shook his head. "They don't have to keep doing this."

"Of course they don't *have* to — they do it because they want to."

Charles sighed. "I guess so. I still wish they wouldn't." He finished reading the letter, folded it neatly, and replaced it in the envelope. "Come on, let me dump this stuff in my room."

"Nice house," Buddy said, looking around.

"Yeah, I like it, too." Charles crossed the living

room, opening his bedroom door. "This is my room."

"Not bad." Buddy came in, checking the walls, nodding. "Not bad at all. Oh, God." He indicated the Crawford College banner over Charles' bed. "Should I throw up now or later?"

"Bathroom's in there," Charles said, pointing.

"It's okay, I'll wait." He frowned at the poster on the back door. "Katharine *Hepburn*?"

"I like her."

"Yeah, but all dressed like that?"

"Why not?"

"Not in *my* room."

"Maybe on the *posters*," Charles said.

"Oh, funny." Buddy dropped his knapsack on Charles' neatly made bed, then grinned sheepishly. "Or, not so funny."

Charles laughed.

"*Depressing*, even." Buddy flopped down on the floor, doing a few push-ups.

"Trying to get a couple of muscles?" Charles asked.

Buddy shrugged. "More you exercise the better." He lifted his left arm behind his back, lowering himself slowly with his right arm. "I can just about do them one-handed."

"Oh yeah?" Charles asked. "I can do them with my *eyes* closed."

Buddy frowned, stopping in the middle of the push-up.

"Joke," Charles said.

"Oh," Buddy said, and finished the push-up. "I knew that."

"And you say *I* need help?"

"Hey, Charles!" Jason yelled. "You home yet?"

"In here, Jason!" Charles called back. "He's the youngest," he explained to Buddy.

"Guess what?" Jason asked, skidding into the room. "In baseball today, I hit two — " he stopped. "Oh, hi."

"Jason, this is my friend Buddy, from school."

"From *California*," Buddy said, standing up and grinning at Jason. "Hey, Bucko."

"Hey, Beachboy," Jason said.

"We're going to work on our English papers," Charles explained. "Right, Buddy?"

"Oh, yeah. Definitely." He draped his arm around Charles' shoulders. "I'm kind of like a tutor."

"Sure," Jason said. "Hey, Charles, is it okay if I go play football with the guys?"

"Which guys?"

"You know, from school. David, Gary, Luke — all those guys."

"Where?"

"Down at the field. Where you think?"

"Well, okay," Charles said. "But be home by five-thirty — I think your mother wants to eat early tonight. Oh, and Jason?"

Jason stopped halfway out of the room.

"Don't wear your school clothes."

"Can I wear church clothes?"

Charles grinned. "No."

"What a parent," Buddy said when he was gone.

"I am not."

"Not much you're not."

Charles flipped a pillow at him, heading out to the kitchen.

"What do you want to eat?" he asked, opening the refrigerator door.

"Whatever." Buddy grinned. "As much as you have."

"That's what I figured." Charles took out two Cokes, handing Buddy one. He bent to search the lower shelves, coming up with two oranges.

"What, are they into health food here?"

"Sort of." Charles opened one of the cupboards, taking out a bag of corn chips. "Sometimes."

They ended up out at the table in the living room, books open, Charles actually working on his paper, Buddy eating.

"You hear the joke about Michael Jackson and Richard Pryor?" Buddy asked.

Charles kept writing. "Yes."

"Oh." Buddy frowned. "Really?"

"Yeah." Charles looked over. "Aren't you going to do any work at all?"

"Nope."

"It's supposed to be two thousand words. Have you started yours yet?"

"Nope."

"Then, how're you going to — "

"Sunday night," Buddy said. "That's how I always do stuff."

Charles shook his head. "I don't see how you can do that. I know I'd get an ulcer."

"That," Buddy helped himself to more chips, "is what makes us different, Charles."

Charles grinned. "The only thing?"

Buddy nodded. "Except for our hair color."

"Yeah, I use Preference."

"There you go," Buddy said. "I use Clairol."

The front door opened and two space mutants came in, scanning the room, ray guns out and leveled. One of them nodded at Charles, and the mutants went into the kitchen, Charles going back to his paper.

"That wasn't weird?" Buddy asked.

"No. *Weird* is when he comes in wearing a cow's head or something."

"That was one of the 'things' you take care of?"

Charles nodded. "Douglas. I think the other one was his friend Norman. It's kind of hard to tell with the masks."

Buddy took some more corn chips. "Can't imagine why."

Lila was the last one home, wearing what Jason called her "moony" expression. Whenever he said that, Douglas would always yell at him, saying that he shouldn't make fun of the moon like that.

"Charter member, Alexander Morgan Fan Club," Charles said to Buddy.

"Who?"

"Just this guy in her class." Charles put down his pen. "Good day at school, Lila?"

She sighed.

"That means yes," he said to Buddy. "Lila, this is my friend, Buddy."

She snapped out of it. "A friend named Buddy or a friend who is a buddy?"

"Both, ma'am," Buddy said, standing up and bowing low enough to stumble off-balance. "At your service."

70

Lila looked at him, amused. "What a goon machine."

"*Goon* machine?" Buddy said. "I, Buddy Lembeck, heart throb of the Crawford campus, called a *goon* machine?"

"Suits you," Charles said.

"Thanks."

"Charles, are you working hard?" Lila asked. "I mean, can you still — ?"

"Sure," Charles said, putting down his pen. "Let me see where your mother put the car keys."

"And can we pick up — "

"Sure." He turned to Buddy. "You mind?"

"Me?" Buddy asked. "Mind not studying?"

Lila shook her head. "Major goon machine."

"Hey, Charles!" Jason came downstairs, changed into a New York Rangers sweatshirt and old gray sweatpants. "Where you going? Can you give me a ride to the field?"

"Sure. Why not?"

Lila shuddered. "Ride in the car with *that*?"

Charles turned toward the kitchen. "Douglas! Norman! I have to drive over to the mall for a minute. You want to come with me, or wait here?"

"Can you take us to the arcade?" Douglas asked, mask still on, holding three Oreos.

"Well — " Charles looked at Buddy uncertainly. It looked like all of this was going to turn into a major production.

Buddy shrugged. "Whatever."

"You have any quarters I can borrow?" Douglas asked.

Charles grinned. "*Borrow*?" Luckily, Mr. Pembroke was giving him money every week, for him to dole out when the kids used up their allowances, which was usually shortly after they received them. He took two dollars out of his wallet. "Spend them wisely."

Hey!" Jason said. "Can I have some, too?"

"You don't need money to play football."

"It gets hot," Jason said. "I might need ice cream to revive myself."

Charles gave him a dollar.

"*While* you're at it," Lila said, with a very charming smile.

"How much?" Charles asked.

"Five?" Lila asked, sounding as though she would settle for three.

Charles gave her five and started to put his wallet away. Good thing Mr. Pembroke wasn't strict about money.

"You know," Buddy said, "if you're going to hand out money. . . ."

Charles laughed. "No way, goon machine."

Chapter Eight

As the semester went on, Buddy was more likely to sleep through class and borrow Charles' notes.

"English meets at one-o'clock," Charles said. "How can you sleep through that?"

"I keep telling you, Charles." Buddy yawned and looked pitiful. "I'm a growing boy. I need my rest."

"It's because you stay up all night."

"I have insomnia."

"Party disease, more likely."

"I know," Buddy said sadly. "The doctor tells me I have only seven-and-a-half more semesters to live."

"Life is rough," Charles said, and gave him his notes to photocopy.

So he wasn't surprised to walk into psychology the week after midterms and not see Buddy in their usual row. He stopped in the aisle, looking around to be sure. No, nowhere in sight. There had probably been a major dorm party the night before. That meant —

"Excuse me," someone behind him said, and Charles realized that he was blocking the aisle.

"Oh, sorry." He moved out of the way and smelled light, flowery perfume as Gwendolyn Pierce walked by, taking a seat up near the front, three boys and a girl joining her.

Gwendolyn Pierce. He had just spoken to Gwendolyn Pierce. Buddy was going to be insanely jealous — and would probably never sleep through class again.

Wow. Charles sat down, aware that he was grinning foolishly. What a nice voice she had.

"Hey, Charles," a guy he knew from Buddy's dorm said, sitting next to him. "What's up?"

"Uh — " Charles coughed, getting rid of the foolish grin. "Nothing much."

"How much you want to bet Lembeck's sleeping through again?"

"Ten to one," Charles agreed, and as class started, tried to concentrate on taking notes, glancing up at the long, blonde hair near the front as little as possible. No more than twice a minute, say. Once, three times. Buddy wasn't going to have very good notes to photocopy this time.

"I missed it?" Buddy said at lunch, as jealous as Charles had anticipated. "I don't believe it!"

Charles picked up his pizza. "We talked for about ten minutes," he said, taking a bite.

"I don't believe it."

"At length," Charles said.

"What did she really say? 'Can I borrow a pencil, kid?' "

Charles grinned sheepishly. "She said, 'Excuse me.' And I said, 'Oh, sorry.'"

"That's it?"

Charles nodded.

"That's it, huh?" Buddy moved his jaw, considering that. "Not bad," he said finally. "It's a lot better than I'm doing."

Charles imitated Buddy's inevitable modest shrug when it came to women. "What can I say?"

Coming home, Charles automatically checked the counter near the refrigerator to see where everyone was. Usually Mrs. Pembroke left him a note. He didn't see one, so he continued to his room, putting his books on the desk. He could hear the typewriter in the study and decided to go and ask.

Mrs. Pembroke was in there, typing furiously, several crumpled pieces of paper lying near the trashcan. Presumably, some had gone in. He knocked on the doorjamb.

"Charles, hi," she said, sounding distracted. "How was your day?"

"Fine, thank you."

"Did you get that paper back?"

He nodded.

"How'd you do?"

He allowed himself a sheepish grin. "A."

She shook her head, impressed. "Looks like you're heading for a 4.0 this semester."

"I sure hope so." He shifted his weight, hands in pockets. "Any of the kids around?"

Mrs. Pembroke nodded. "Lila's here with Terri — I think they're watching television. Jason has soccer practice, and Douglas should be along any minute now."

Charles also nodded. "Is there anything you want me to do this afternoon?"

"Well, I — " She hesitated. "Do you have plans?"

"No," he assured her. "I mean, there's a basketball game I wouldn't mind going to tonight, but I'm not doing anything this afternoon."

"Hannah had to leave early. Do you think — " Mrs. Pembroke frowned. "I really hate to ask you to do this sort of thing."

He shrugged. "No problem."

"Could you vacuum the living room?"

"Sure. Is there anything else?"

"No, I — " She sighed. "Well, sort of."

He paused.

"I really hate to ask you to do errands, Charles."

"It's no problem."

"Well." She went across the room to her pocketbook, taking a little yellow slip out of her wallet. "Would you mind going by the dry cleaners and picking up some things for me? I'd ask Stan to do it, but they close at four-thirty."

Charles took the slip and the money she handed him, putting them in his pocket. "Sure thing."

"Thank you, Charles." She shook her head. "I really don't know what we'd do without you."

He smiled self-consciously.

Hearing music as he passed the den, he stuck his head in and saw Lila and her friend Terri dancing to a Michael Jackson video on MTV.

"*Charles*," Lila said, hands going to her hips as her friend giggled.

"Sorry." He pushed away from the door.

"He's so *cute*," Terri was saying as he went down the hall.

The vacuum cleaner was kept in the linen closet and he took it out, doing the stairs before starting the living room. He was working on the fireplace hearth — it got really messy these days since it was colder and Mr. Pembroke was lighting fires at night — when Douglas tapped him on the shoulder. Charles jumped, but recovered himself.

"Do you have to do work all afternoon?" Douglas yelled over the noise.

"Some!" Charles yelled back. "Why?"

"Because —" Douglas stopped. "Why don't you just turn it off?"

"Oh, right." Charles flipped the switch and it was quiet. "Why?" he asked in a normal voice.

"Can you give me a ride to the library? I have to do a report for school."

"Do you need to be there long?"

Douglas shook his head. "Just to get some books."

"Wait until I finish here, then. I'll drop you off on my way to the dry cleaner's." He turned the vacuum cleaner back on.

"Thanks, Charles!" Douglas yelled over the noise, and Charles nodded.

After he'd finished taking Douglas to the library and picking up the clothes, he had just enough time to read some economics before dinner.

"Hot date tonight?" Jason asked as Charles glanced at his watch.

"No, he's going to a stupid basketball game," Douglas said, trying to camouflage the meatloaf on his plate so Mr. Pembroke would think he had eaten it.

"Basketball? Wow!" Jason said. "Can I come? Please?"

"It's Charles' night off," Mrs. Pembroke reminded him. "You can go some other time."

Jason picked at his meatloaf, looking very disappointed.

"Hey, I don't mind if you come," Charles said. "That is," he added hastily, "if your parents don't."

"It *is* a school night," Mr. Pembroke said.

"Oh, Dad. Please?"

"I don't think it's a good idea. Charles probably has plans after the game."

"Well, not really," Charles said. *Not officially, anyway.* "I just told Buddy and some other guys I'd meet them there."

"Well," Mrs. Pembroke said, "I still think that you would probably rather have a night to yourself."

He would, kind of, but Jason looked so disappointed that Charles shook his head. "I'd be glad if he came — it'll be fun."

"Really?" Jason asked, his parents' doubt contagious.

"Sure. We're playing Conn College — it should be good."

"Can I go, Mom? Dad?" Jason looked from one parent to the other. "Please?"

"Well," Mrs. Pembroke hesitated. "If Charles really doesn't mind. . . ."

So, he ended up bringing Jason along — which meant that he got to borrow the station wagon. He'd tried to talk Douglas into tagging along, but Douglas had steadfastly refused, with the opinion that basketball was for the "physically efficient-intellectually deficient" set. "Except for you, Charles," he'd added.

Buddy, waiting outside the gym, looked briefly surprised, but recovered himself.

"Hey, Bucko," he said. "You like basketball?"

"Yeah!" Jason said.

Charles smiled, reaching down to ruffle up Jason's hair.

"Sam and Danny are saving seats for us," Buddy said.

Charles glanced at Jason. "Will there be enough room?"

Buddy shrugged. "If there isn't, we'll move." He flashed his student ID at the ticket taker; Charles flashed his own, then bought Jason a ticket.

Jason pulled on his sleeve. "Is it okay?" he whispered. "I didn't know it was going to cost anything."

"Your father gave it to me — don't worry."

The seats Sam and Danny had saved were in the bleachers, so there was plenty of room.

"Yo, Charles," Sam said as they sat down. "How's it going?"

"Not bad." He put his hand on Jason's shoulder. "This is Jason."

"Hi, kid," Sam said.

Danny just nodded, his mouth full of popcorn. "Little brother?" he asked when he'd swallowed.

Charles hesitated, then saw that Jason was beaming, considering that a huge compliment. "Yeah," he said. "Pretty much."

After the game — which Crawford won 85–79 — Charles knew that Buddy and the guys probably wanted to go to Harry's for pizza, but they were hesitant about saying so in front of Jason. And since Harry's was very rowdy, it wasn't the kind of place he would take a ten-year-old.

"You guys going to Harry's?" Charles asked.

"Um, well — " Buddy glanced at Sam and Danny, then back. "What do *you* want to do?"

"I figured Jason and I might go by Baskin-Robbins or something."

The boys looked relieved.

"You want to come by later?" Danny said. "We'll probably still be there."

Charles shrugged. "Maybe. I'll have to play it by ear."

The boys nodded.

"Catch you later," Sam said. "Glad you came, Jason."

Jason's grin was huge. "It was great!"

Once they were in the car, he lost some of his enthusiasm.

"Charles?"

"Mmmm?" Charles asked, trying to find the ignition key in the darkness. "You like the game?"

"Yeah."

"Good."

"Charles?"

He found the key and started the engine. "What?"

"If you want, you can just drop me off. If you'd rather go with your friends, I mean."

Charles glanced over. "*You're* my friend, aren't you?"

"Well — yeah. But it's different."

"No, it isn't. I feel like going and having ice cream with you."

"Yeah, but Mom said — "

"Look." Charles turned the engine off. "If I didn't want to go, I'd say so. And right now, what I want to do is go order the biggest sundae they have."

"But — well, Mom and Dad say that we shouldn't get on your nerves. Not to get in your way when you're doing college stuff."

"I *like* it when you get in my way," Charles said and, saying it, he realized that it was true. "When I was your age, I was the only one in the house and it got lonely sometimes. *Lots* of times. I really *wanted* brothers and sisters — older, younger, whatever. Just to have them around. Not to be the only one who thought Christmas was a big deal." He shrugged, embarrassed by what was turning into a speech. "That kind of stuff."

"So you don't mind?"

"No," Charles said firmly. "Okay?"

Jason nodded.

"Okay." Charles started the engine and glanced over his back shoulder before pulling out.

"You're as good as any of those guys on our team," Jason said as they drove.

"You think?" Charles signaled right at the parking lot exit. "They looked pretty good to me."

Jason shook his head. "You're about ten times better."

"Well, I don't know," Charles said, grinning. "Maybe."

"How come you didn't try out?"

"Takes too much time."

"What, you mean because of us?"

"No." Charles slowed for a red light. "Too much studying. They practice two or three hours every day. I can't afford to waste that much time."

"You think basketball's a waste?"

"No, I — " Charles frowned, trying to explain it. "I mean, I like it, and I played in high school and everything, and I like shooting around with you, but — I don't know. I guess school just seems more important now."

"Gross," Jason said.

"Yeah. Kind of." Charles accelerated as the light turned green. "But right now, I like school better. I don't know, I guess you go through phases, you know?"

"*I'm* never going to like school better."

"You never know, you might."

"You think Douglas will ever like sports better than school?"

Charles had to grin, imagining that. "I don't know," he said. "He might."

Jason laughed. "Boy, wait 'til I tell him! He'll be really mad."

Charles also laughed, picturing Douglas as a big, swaggering football center, wearing his astronaut helmet instead of a regular one. They were near Baskin-Robbins now and he signaled left, checking for traffic before turning in and guiding the car into a parking place. In high school, he had been something of a speed demon when he got to borrow his parents' car. But when he was driving around with someone like Jason — well, things seemed different. He even wore a seatbelt now.

"Charles?"

"What?"

"Did you mean it when you said I was pretty much your little brother?"

Charles smiled and reached over to give him a playful shove. "Yeah," he said. "I did."

Chapter Nine

He got to the dining hall before Buddy the next day, and decided to join the line anyway. Buddy would catch up to him. He pushed his tray along, selecting one of those awful hamburgers, then moved on to the desserts. Buddy was a bad influence on him. He took a piece of cake and after thinking about it, added two more. There was ice cream, too, so he put a large dish on his tray, noticing the single cup of yogurt on the tray next to his. Strawberry. He glanced over to smile at the girl — it *had* to be a girl — and was horrified to see Gwendolyn Pierce, as beautiful as ever in a light gray sweater and well-fitting jeans.

"Nutritious lunch," she said, indicating his tray.

"I — " He couldn't get any words to come out. "I mean — yeah," he said finally, feeling himself blush. *Blush.* When was the last time he had blushed? "Um —" he glanced at her tray — "*boring* lunch."

She smiled and he felt dizzy. "Yeah, I suppose it is."

She was about to turn away and he had to do something, say something. "Um, you're in my psych class, aren't you?" He closed his eyes. Talk about original.

She nodded. "I thought you looked familiar."

She'd *noticed* him? "Well, same class and all," he said, and wanted to kick himself for being such an inane jerk.

"Gwendolyn, over here!" someone called from a table near the wall.

"Well," Gwendolyn said. "I guess I'd better. . ."

"Yeah. Uh, nice talking to you."

She smiled again. "You, too."

He stood there, holding his tray, watching her walk across the cafeteria. Her tray! What a jerk he was, he could have offered to take her tray. He'd never get a chance like that again. Shaking his head, he carried his own tray over to the table where he and Buddy and whoever else was around usually sat.

"Hey," Buddy said, showing up a couple of minutes later. "What's up?"

Charles was about to tell him about Gwendolyn, but Buddy was still talking.

"I asked Carol and Wendy to have lunch with us," he was saying. "You mind?"

"How come you never ask *me* first?" Charles asked.

"I don't know. I mean — you want me to tell them not to?" Buddy asked, his voice genuinely disappointed.

Charles smiled. "No. I just meant in general."

"You sure?"

"Yeah."

"It's not too late — I can see them over there."

Charles laughed. "Don't worry about it."

"They're really nice."

Charles nodded, looking across the cafeteria at Gwendolyn Pierce sitting with four guys and another girl.

"It's still not too late," Buddy said.

"I *want* to have lunch with them."

Buddy sat down, looking very relieved. "Good."

Charles was in his room, reading the highlighted notes in his psychology book, when Mrs. Pembroke knocked on the door.

"Studying hard?" she asked.

He nodded, running a tired hand through his hair. One of these days, college was going to make him need glasses.

"Do you want me to come back later?"

"No, it's okay." He pushed away from the desk. "I mean, I could use a break." He stood up, stretching. "Something you need me to do?"

She smiled. "No. I know you need time to study. How's it coming?"

"Well — " He looked at the psychology book, where he was three chapters ahead of the class, his finished English paper sitting neatly in a folder, his completed French translation on top of it. "Pretty well, I guess."

"*Very* well, I'd say."

He shrugged, embarrassed. "How's the newspaper going?"

"Well — pretty well," she said. "I think it'll be easier once Fletcher breaks down and retires."

"It sounds like he has a pretty serious problem."

"Only before performances." She smiled wryly. "I think he does it to get out of things he knows he's going to hate."

"So you get stuck with all the experimental stuff?"

"Exactly." She indicated the new poster of Ingrid Bergman. "Very nice."

"Thanks."

"I know it's a little early, but I wanted to ask what you're going to do about Thanksgiving. Are you going home?"

"Well — " He bit his lip. His parents were expecting him, but if the Pembrokes wanted — "Well, I was sort of planning on it, but if you need me to — "

"Of course not," she said. "I mean, you'd be welcome to stay here — we'd love to have you, but I'm sure your parents would be very disappointed."

"Yeah. Kind of."

"You must be looking forward to it."

"Well, yeah," he said. "But it seems kind of strange, too."

"The first time you go home when you've been away always is. But the minute you sit down, and your mother has all of your favorite foods — it'll seem as if you never left."

"I guess so," Charles said. He *hoped* so. Sometimes, like late at night right before his midterms, or when he got a letter, he felt really homesick, but other times, he didn't think about it much. Or the phone would ring, and it would be his parents, and he would wish that he was back there, but other times, he was so glad to be in college and doing his own thing that — well, it was weird.

"It will be strange for your parents, too," Mrs. Pembroke said. "Having you home, I mean."

He nodded.

"But, good."

He nodded again.

"And don't worry about staying here until the last minute. As soon as you get out of classes, and can get a — what are you going to do, take a train? The bus?"

"The bus, probably."

"Well, make sure you go before late Wednesday — it'll be mobbed otherwise, what with everyone going home."

He nodded, that particular problem not having occurred to him.

"Are you all set for money? Because if you aren't, we can — "

"Oh, I'm fine," he said. "I mean, thank you, but I'm all set."

Mrs. Pembroke nodded. "I figured you would be, but the offer is still there."

"What are all of you going to do?"

"Go to the children's grandmother's house, I expect. She lives in Darien, where Stan grew up."

Charles nodded. "Sounds good."

"I love Thanksgiving," Mrs. Pembroke agreed. "Well." She moved back towards the door. "You should get back to your studying."

Charles sighed. "Yeah."

"Well, don't push yourself *too* hard. It's not good for you."

"Probably not." He sat back down at his desk, staring at the yellow and green highlights. "Mrs. Pembroke?"

She turned.

"Thank you."

"This weather is a major drag," Buddy said, zipping his jacket as they left their psychology class. "I talked to my parents last night and they said that the surf's been really great."

"What, even your *parents* surf?"

"No. But my brother Mickey does, so they keep track."

"So they'll know when to worry."

"Right. Oh, hold on a minute." Buddy stopped and bent down to tie his Topsiders. "I don't know why you Easterners wear these stupid things — they never stay tied."

Charles looked down at his feet. "Mine do."

"Yours would." Buddy straightened up. "I swear, I'm tempted to make double knots."

"If you think they're so stupid, how come you bought a pair?"

Buddy shrugged. "You know how it is — do as the natives do."

"What do you do in California, wear *thongs*?"

"Hey, they do the job."

"Which job is that?"

"Get you from one place to the other, what else?"

"What else," Charles said. "Besides, I thought

all you guys did was cruise around in your cars."

"Hey, we have to walk from the parking lot, don't we?" He gaves Charles a light punch on the shoulder. "Come on, get with it."

"Sorry."

"Hey, look!" This time, Buddy's punch was more urgent. "Look over there!"

Charles turned and saw Gwendolyn Pierce walking nearby, with a boy and a girl from their class. Quickly, he looked away, feeling himself flush. *Again*?

"Boy," Buddy said, "she really is something else. I mean, I can't *believe* how — "

She was passing them now and Buddy coughed.

"So, *anyway*," he said, "there I was, at the top of the — "

Gwendolyn smiled at them. "Hi."

"H-hi," Charles said.

Buddy just stared.

As she went past them, Buddy hit Charles in the ribs.

"Hey, ow!" Charles moved away. "Cut that out!"

"Did you see that, Charles? She said 'hi' to us! Gwendolyn Pierce said 'hi' to us!"

Charles grinned. "To *us*? Looked more like she said 'hi' to *me*."

"What, a loser like you?" Buddy shook his head. "Your brain must be out to lunch, pal."

"At least I have one *some* of the time."

"Oh, funny," Buddy said. "Real funny. You have a professional write your jokes these days?"

"Yeah," Charles said. "Does it show?"

"Oh, wow, funny twice in a row. The flags must be at half-mast."

"If you want," Charles said, "I'll see if they can write you some jokes, too. You *need* them."

"Look who's Mr. Confident all of the sudden." Buddy squinted ahead of them at Gwendolyn going into the Student Center. He looked at Charles. "You really think she was saying 'hi' to you?"

"I don't know." Charles shrugged, suddenly much less certain. "Maybe she's just a friendly person."

"Maybe," Buddy said doubtfully.

After he got home from classes and played a little pick-up basketball with Buddy and some other guys, Charles went over to check the list. If there was one.

He found a note on the refrigerator, written in blue Magic Marker, brief and to the point. "Jason, Douglas — home right after school. Lila — home after makeup algebra test. Leaves? Thanks, Mrs. P." That last meant that she wanted him to try and get the last of the leaves in the yard raked up. He'd gotten Jason and Douglas to help him with the first batch a few weeks ago, but since then, many more had fallen, and it had rained often enough to make trying to rake a waste of time. Since it had been dry for a few days now, this was probably a good afternoon to get the job done.

He changed into jeans and an old sweatshirt with a faded U Penn across the front and headed for the garage to get a rake. Jason and Douglas were in the kitchen, fighting over what was left of the cookies and he paused, ending the fight by taking the last two cookies and putting them into his mouth.

"Charles!" Jason said. "That's not fair!"

"I'm bigger than you," Charles said.

Jason and Douglas looked at each other.

"It's fair," Douglas said.

"Yeah," Jason agreed.

"I'm going outside to do some raking. How about you guys give me a hand?"

"No way," Jason said. "I'm going to play football."

"And I'm watching *Star Trek*," Douglas agreed.

"And *I'm* bigger than you are," Charles said, looming over them.

The boys looked at each other again.

"We'll help," Jason said.

With the three of them working together, the raking went fairly quickly, Charles dividing the yard into four sections and doing them one at a time. Douglas and Jason would help him stuff the leaves into a garbage bag and he would lug it down to the empty lot a few houses down.

"Hey, look!" Jason pointed with his rake. "There's *Lila*!"

They all turned to see Lila coming up the driveway.

"Busy?" Charles asked, putting on an evil smile.

She stopped. "Oh, no. I mean — I can't, I have to —"

"That's not fair," Jason said. "Just 'cause you're

a girl doesn't mean you can get out of things. Right, Charles?"

"Right," Charles said.

"Oh, come on," Lila begged. "I *can't*. I said I'd call Sarah, and then I have to — "

"*We* had to do stuff, too," Douglas said.

"Yeah, but it's *important*," Lila said.

"Well, okay." Charles started raking again. "If you don't want to help us, or be a good sport, or — "

She sighed. "Okay, okay. Can I at least go in and change?"

Charles looked at Jason and Douglas. "What do you think?"

"Maybe just this once," Douglas said.

"If it never happens again," Jason added.

"Okay then." He turned back to Lila. "You can change."

"If I don't come out right away, will you come after me?"

He nodded.

"Okay, okay," she said grumpily. "I'll be out in a minute." She returned in a light blue sweatshirt and jeans, looking at the leaves distastefully. "There aren't enough rakes," she said and turned to go back inside.

"No problem," Charles said, catching her by the shoulder and spinning her around. "You can use mine, or you can put leaves into the bags."

She looked at the rake and the bags, deciding. "Do I have to use my hands?"

"Unless you can do it with your feet," Jason said.

Lila sighed deeply, and took the rake Charles was offering. "Where do I start?"

With four of them working, it went even faster, and soon, they were raking up the last section.

"Hey, look out!" Jason said and stuffed some leaves down Lila's back.

"Charles!" she protested, trying to get them out.

Charles picked up Jason and tossed him into the pile they had made, Douglas and Lila covering him with more leaves.

"Hey, that's not fair," Jason said, struggling. "Three against one's not fair!"

"It is if we get *Charles*," Lila said and they all jumped on him.

Teams changed more than once, instinctively — everyone jumping on Charles, then everyone going after Douglas, then after Lila again — and finally, laughing too hard to continue, they all ended up on the grass, covered with leaves and twigs.

"What a, what a mess," Charles said, out of breath.

"You mean — " Lila was out of breath, too. "We have to do all of this over again?"

Charles nodded, brushing the leaves off his sweatshirt. He heard Jason behind him and turned to catch him in the act of trying to start the fight again.

"Once is funny," he said. "Twice is a pain."

Jason dropped the leaves and picked up his rake with an angelic smile. "Who, me?"

They were just finishing up when Mr. Pembroke pulled into the driveway.

"Hey, Dad's home!" Douglas said. "Can we quit now?"

"In a minute," Charles said. "We're almost done."

Mr. Pembroke got out of the car, and Charles said, "Hi, Mr. Pembroke," among a chorus of "Hi, Dad" 's.

"Hi, guys." He surveyed the yard. "Looks good."

"Boy, did we work," Jason said. "And Charles wouldn't do *anything*."

"Yeah," Douglas said, nodding. "He was lying on the grass, giving us orders and everything."

"All afternoon," Lila agreed.

Mr. Pembroke laughed. "Well, from the looks of the yard, he's a pretty good supervisor." He lifted his briefcase to his other hand to rest his right hand on Jason's shoulder. "How about we all knock off for the day and go in and get something to eat?"

"Food!" Jason said, running for the door.

Douglas looked at his watch. "*Battlestar Galactica*'s on, too."

"Freedom," Lila said, letting her rake fall and heading for the house.

Since there were still a few leaves, Charles stayed to rake them up.

"I meant you, too, Charles," Mr. Pembroke said.

"But — I mean, there are still a few — "

"So what?" Mr. Pembroke said. "Gives the yard character. Come on, let's go in."

Charles hesitated.

Then he dropped the rake.

Chapter Ten

There was a huge campus party the next Tuesday night, which Charles missed because the Pembrokes had to go out, and when he walked into psychology class on Wednesday, class attendance was sparse at best. Apparently, the entire campus was recovering from the party. There were maybe fifty people in the auditorium and their professor let the class out early. As he closed his notebook and reached for his sweater, Charles noticed Gwendolyn Pierce leaving, alone for once.

If he didn't talk to her now, he never would.

He yanked the sweater on and hurried to the door, timing it so they would be leaving at the same time.

"Hi," he said.

"Oh, hi." She smiled. "How are you?"

"I — " That question wasn't what he had expected. "I mean, fine. How are you?"

"Fine."

He held the outside door for her, wondering where to go from there.

"Uh, pretty quiet around here today," he said.

She nodded. "It was quite a party last night. Did you go?"

"Well — no," he said. "I kind of had to work."

"Oh?" she asked, sounding interested. "What do you do?"

"Well, I — " Should he tell her the truth? Yeah. "I live with a family off-campus and I had to baby-sit last night."

"Oh," she said, sounding even more interested. "Do you enjoy it?"

"Babysitting?"

"Well, that, too. I meant, living off-campus and all."

"Oh. Well, actually, I do," he said. "They're really nice kids."

"It must be different to commute."

He nodded. "I miss out on some things, I guess, but it makes it easier to study."

"I'm sure," she said.

Did she sound turned off? No, not as far as he could tell. She sounded as if she *liked* the idea even.

"Well," she said, slowing as they got to the English building. "I have a class now."

"Oh," Charles said. "I mean, you do?"

She indicated the building.

"Ah," he said. "Well, it was nice talking to you."

"You, too."

She was leaving, he had to say something, had to think of — "Uh, my name's Charles."

"Hi, Charles," she said. "I'm Gwendolyn."

"Pretty," he said, then blushed. Blushing *again*? "The name, I mean. I mean — "

"I think I know what you mean," she said. "See you later."

"Uh, yeah. You, too."

After classes that day, he and Buddy went running, doing almost four miles on the Crawford cross country course.

"Good workout," Buddy said in the locker room, drying his hair from the shower.

Charles nodded. "Guess I miss sports more than I thought I would."

"Speaking of things you miss, there's a party at Psi Upsilon this weekend. You coming?"

"I don't know. It depends on what's going on."

"You get stuck there almost every weekend."

Charles shrugged. "It's not so bad."

"You missed a great one last night."

"I heard," Charles said and blushed. Yet *again*? Unreal.

"So you should come to this one. I know some of the guys in the frat and they said it was going to be really good."

"Yeah." Would Gwendolyn be there? Yeah, probably. With about six different dates.

"Whole *bunches* of girls are going to be there," Buddy said.

"I'm sure."

"Or, I could look around for some dates. You want me to look around?"

"Buddy, I can get my own dates."

"I know, I know," Buddy said. "You get *good* dates. I just mean in case I run into — twins or something."

His voice was too innocent and Charles turned to look at him.

"*Twins*, Buddy?"

"Yeah, you should see them!" Buddy said enthusiastically. "Long red hair, big blue eyes, they're really — "

"Don't tell me," Charles said. "Let me guess. You invited them to lunch."

"Well — yeah."

Charles groaned.

"Well, I worry about you," Buddy said. "Stuck out at some house all the time. I'm just trying to help."

Charles sighed. "Yeah, I know."

"You'll see, it'll be great. You're going to love these girls."

"What, are you my mother?"

"Your mother?" As always, Buddy was physically taken aback. "Charles, you — "

"— cut you to the quick, I know," Charles finished the sentence for him. "Look, I have to get going. I have to drive Douglas to the orthodontist."

"Okay," Buddy said. "But at least have lunch with them, okay? I know you'll — "

"Buddy."

"Please?"

Charles sighed. "Okay, but this is the last time."

"It is," Buddy said. "I promise."

Charles grinned wryly. "Somehow, I'm not going to count on that."

Watching television that night, Charles noticed that Jason, Douglas, and Lila were all in the room watching, too. Kind of nice. When he'd first moved in, he'd be lucky if he could get *two* of them to agree on a show, let alone all three.

"We all enjoying ourselves?" he asked.

"This is a stupid movie," Douglas said, wearing 3-D glasses. "None of it could happen in real life."

"So what?" Charles asked. "Shut up and pass me the popcorn."

"Does it have butter on it?" Lila asked.

"Well — a little," Charles admitted. "Not enough to make any difference."

"How come you always put butter on it, Charles? I mean, the oil's bad enough." She took a large handful, anyway.

"Diet destroyed," Douglas said.

Lila sighed and put it back.

"Don't put it back!" Jason protested. "Not after you've gotten germs all over it!"

"I don't have germs."

"Yeah, you do. Gross girl germs. All kinds of —"

"Charles, make him stop," Lila said.

Charles leaned over and cuffed him. "Cut it out."

"It's true!" Jason said, pushing the popcorn away.

"That's not the point," Charles said patiently. "Don't —"

"What?" Lila asked. "You think I have germs, Charles?"

"I didn't say that."

"Yeah, you did! I mean, it's not like —"

"Everyone has germs," Douglas remarked, taking a handful of popcorn and washing it down with milk. "The air is full of bacteria. Like, a person's mouth has more germs than a dog's."

"What if the person *is* a dog?" Jason asked.

Lila hit him.

"Hey, cut it out!" Charles sat between them to break up the fight. "Be nice."

"Be *nice*?" Lila said, and she and Jason laughed.

"Boy, I'm terrified," Jason said.

"You should be." Charles flexed his muscles.

"Help!" Jason squirmed away in pretended fear. "Corporal punishment! Mom, Dad, help!"

"Hey, shut up," Douglas said. "I'm trying to watch this."

They all grinned at him.

"Thought you said it was stupid," Jason reminded him.

"Doesn't mean I can't watch it."

"Yeah, but you said —"

"Charles, will you make him —"

Mr. Pembroke stuck his head in. "Everything okay in here?"

They all sat back politely and smiled at him.

"Fine, Dad," Douglas said.

"*Fun* even," Lila said.

Charles nodded several times. "Absolutely."

"Well. I'm glad." He lifted an eyebrow at Jason. "Don't yell, it makes your mother and me nervous."

"Me, yell?" Jason asked.

"Must have been our imagination." He turned to leave. "Well, enjoy yourselves."

"That's just what we're doing," Charles said, "right?"

Lila put a weak hand to her head as though swooning, Jason grimaced, and Douglas crossed his eyes.

"We sure are," Charles said.

For the next few minutes, they all watched quietly, eating popcorn.

"There are bacteria everywhere," Douglas said. "The only reason we aren't sick all the time is because our bodies build up immunities to — "

"Douglas!" they all said at once.

"Who, me?" he asked and subsided.

"What a lot of fun we're having," Charles said. "Right, guys?"

"Charles!" they all said.

"You don't like the twins?" Buddy asked as they played one-on-one in one of the Crawford gyms. "I don't believe you don't like them."

"They're okay." Charles faked left and drove right, past Buddy for a lay-up. "They're just not my type, that's all."

Buddy took the rebound and dribbled out to the foul line. "They're beautiful girls, what else do you need?"

"I don't know." Charles reached in to steal the ball and Buddy spun away, still dribbling. "I kind of like it when people know how to do more than giggle."

"They're good at giggling," Buddy said and tried a jump shot. Both of them moved in for the rebound, struggled briefly, and Charles ended up with the ball, taking it out to the foul line.

"They're very good at giggling," he agreed. "I've had a headache ever since."

Buddy slapped at the ball, knocking it free, but Charles recovered it and kept dribbling.

"You're too picky," Buddy said, guarding him.

"You're too accepting," Charles said, moving right, then left, trying to shake him. It didn't work, and he faked right, then stepped back and threw a quick jump shot.

Buddy sighed, catching it as it swished through the net, and taking it out. "Can't you ever miss?"

"I miss all the time."

"Not often enough." Buddy drove for the basket, muscling his way through, and made the shot, Charles fouling him in the process. "My ball."

"What do you mean, your ball?"

"You fouled me — I get the ball."

"Not where I come from."

"Yeah, well, look at where you come from."

Charles grabbed the ball, did two spin dribbles, and tossed up a left hook for another basket. He grinned at Buddy. "At least we learn how to play there."

"*That's* for sure." Buddy caught the ball and dribbled back out to the foul line in order to try again.

Later, when they were getting changed, Buddy snapped his fingers.

"Laura Anderson!" he said. "I *know* you'd like her."

"Oh, yeah?" Charles buttoned his shirt. "What makes you so sure?"

"The girl never giggled in her life. I mean, we're talking *librarian* here."

"I never said I wanted a librarian." Charles unzipped his pants to tuck in his shirt. "Besides, some librarians are nice."

"Oh, give me a break."

"My *mother's* a librarian."

Buddy lost his grin. "Really? Hey, sorry."

"I'm kidding." He pulled his watch out of his locker to check the time.

"You have to get going?"

"Yeah. I promised Mrs. Pembroke I'd cook dinner tonight."

Buddy's grin returned. "What are you making?"

"I don't know. Coq au vin or something."

"Yeah, right."

"I don't know. Hamburgers or something."

"That's what I figured." Buddy zipped up his knapsack. "You get the night off tomorrow?"

"Yeah."

"Then we need dates. You want me to find us dates?"

Charles shook his head.

"You sure? It's not too late."

"I'm sure."

"Look, tell me at lunch tomorrow, okay?" Buddy said. "That's not too late."

Charles laughed. "Okay, I'll tell you then."

The next morning, Buddy didn't show up for psychology, so Charles sat closer to the front. Closer to Gwendolyn Pierce, actually.

She was wearing a white silk shirt, a velvet blazer, and dark designer jeans. The girl looked *good*. Automatically, Charles reached up to straighten his tie. Assuming that Buddy wouldn't show up, he'd dressed pretty carefully himself this morning.

After class, he fell into step with her.

"Hi, Gwendolyn," he said.

"Hi, Charles."

"Pretty good class."

She nodded. "I'm glad we're getting into the more behavioral stuff."

"Yeah, me, too." They were near the English building now and he had better make his move. "Well, I guess you have to go to class."

"Yes," she said.

"Well."

She smiled and started down the walk.

"Um, excuse me —" He winced. Too tentative. "I mean, Gwendolyn?"

"Yes, Charles?"

"I was wondering — would you like to go out with me sometime?"

"Yes," she said.

He blinked. That was easy. "Well. Are you busy tonight?"

"No, not particularly."

"Would you like to go out to dinner, and maybe a movie?"

She nodded. "Why don't you call me later and we can decide what time."

"Okay, that sounds good." He opened his notebook so she could write down the number. What a nice number. "Um, thank you." He closed the book. "I'll call you later then."

"Okay," she said. "Bye, Charles."

"Bye, Gwendolyn." He watched her go, somewhat stunned and very pleased. He had a date with Gwendolyn Pierce. *Tonight*. He stood there grinning, then recovered himself.

Buddy. He could hardly wait to tell Buddy.

Chapter Eleven

"You lucky stiff!" Buddy said as they walked into the house, carrying books so it would look as if they were going to do some work.

"I know," Charles said.

"You are the luckiest of the stiffs!"

"I know."

"Gwendolyn Pierce!"

They looked at each other and grinned.

"Gwendolyn Pierce!" they both said.

As usual, they headed for the kitchen. Charles opened the refrigerator, and taking out two apples, tossed Buddy one.

"Hot," Buddy said, shaking his head. "Hotness *personified*. When God made Gwendolyn Pierce, he knew he was God." He glanced over. "And you asked her out?!"

"Yeah." Charles looked at the apple in his hand, still too excited to eat it. "I don't even know how it happened. All of a sudden, this voice comes out of me, like," he lowered his voice. "'Excuse me, Gwendolyn, would you like to go out sometime?' And, this voice came out of her that said yes!"

Grinning hugely, he took a bite out of the apple.

"Tall," Buddy said grimly. "It's because you're tall, right? Gwendolyn's attracted to tall guys." He slouched against the counter, folding his arms. "I don't have a chance." He looked up. "Okay, where's this family keep its sharp instruments?"

Charles laughed. "It's not worth killing yourself over."

"Oh, I don't want to kill myself." He swiped at Charles with an imaginary knife. "I want to cut off your legs."

Charles laughed, standing a little taller as they walked out to the living room. Lila burst into the house, continuing over to Charles without pausing.

"Charles!" she said.

"Lila!" he said, swooning.

"Alexander Morgan!"

"No," Buddy said, holding out his hand. "Buddy Lembeck."

"Not you, goon machine." She turned back to Charles. "Alexander Morgan is *only* the class president, the best athlete, fabulous-looking, most excellent boy in the eighth grade!"

Charles frowned. "I hate his kind."

"And," Lila paused significantly, "I give you one guess who he asked to help him with his homework tonight."

"Gee, I don't know, Lila." Charles considered that. "Just one guess?" He looked at Buddy. "What do you think, goon machine?"

"I don't know," Buddy said. "I'm racking my brain." He scratched his head, deep in thought. "How much time do I have?"

"*Me!*" Lila said.

Charles and Buddy looked at each other, at Lila, then back at each other, shaking their heads.

"No, no way," Charles said. "Never happen."

"No way," Buddy agreed. "Has to be a mistake."

Charles nodded. "You're out, Lila."

"Nuh-uh," she said. "If Alexander Morgan likes me, then I am most *definitely* in. I'm in," she said more slowly, the fact sinking in. "I'm in!"

They watched her run up the stairs.

"Were we ever that young and immature?" Buddy asked.

"Never." Charles paused. "Gwendolyn Pierce."

They exchanged grins. "Gwendolyn *Pierce!*"

Charles sat down on the couch, very pleased with himself. No wonder Buddy went around being so cocky all the time — it felt *great*.

"So." Buddy sat next to him, biting into his apple. "Where you taking her?"

"Well. . ." Charles swung his legs onto the coffee table. "I thought we'd start off with an intimate dinner at some cozy, little, out-of-the-way — "

Buddy made a game show "Time's up!" noise.

"What?" Charles asked.

"Look. Out of the way is where you go when Aunt Harriet fixes you up with something from the *plant* world. When your date eats *flies*, you go out of the way. *This* girl, you show off."

"Where?"

Buddy thought about that. "A packed restaurant," he decided. "When every guy you know is there."

"Why?"

"So you can go like *this*," Buddy said, crossing the room with his arm around an imaginary girl, winking to boys around the restaurant, gloating furiously. "Hey, guys, how's it going? Look what *I* got —"

"You know what, Buddy?" Charles said. "*This* is why you're going to die alone."

Buddy dropped his arm, returning to the couch. "Okay, okay, you're done with dinner. Now where do you take her?"

"Well —"

Buddy made his "Time's up" buzz. "Here," he said, pointing to the couch. "Right here!" He glanced around the room, nodding. "When you took this job, I thought you were nuts. *Suddenly*, I see the advantages." He lowered his voice. "You bring her back here, she gets one look at how good she thinks you got it. . .and she's all yours!" He shook his head. "You stiff."

Charles also shook his head, standing up. "I don't bring dates back here. I don't think the kids are ready for that yet."

Buddy stared at him. "The *kids*? You don't think the kids. . . ? You're kidding, right?" He looked at Charles, whose expression was perfectly serious. "Are you kidding, or are you turning into Sebastian Cabot?"

"I'm turning *into* someone who has new responsibilities, and needs to be in control of himself." Charles nodded, that argument sounding convincing. "Having Gwendolyn here is no good for my control of himself." He blinked, aware that that had come out wrong, not sure how.

"I don't believe you," Buddy said, still staring. "You know what your problem is? You're too sincere for your own good!"

"Don't call me sincere!"

"Lunatic," Buddy said. "You're a lunatic. Gwendolyn goes after lunatics." He grinned. "I still have a chance."

Mrs. Pembroke came down the stairs with her "I'm in the middle of writing a paragraph" expression. "Charles," she said vaguely.

Charles stood up straighter; Buddy did the same. "Hello, Mrs. Pembroke."

"Charles, I know you had tonight off, but the paper just called and. . .I know it's short notice, but Stan and I'll need you to stay here. I hope that doesn't present a problem."

Charles looked at the floor so she wouldn't see his expression. "No," he said, his voice carefully cheerful. "No problem at all."

Mrs. Pembroke smiled. "Good." She nodded at Buddy. "Hello," she said, and headed back upstairs.

Buddy looked at Charles, and went after her. "Wait."

"No," Charles said, trying to intercept him; Buddy avoided his arm.

Mrs. Pembroke turned. "Yes?"

Buddy gave her a charming smile. "I'm Charles' friend — "

"Oh, no," Charles said, sitting down.

"Yes." Mrs. Pembroke was nodding. "You're the one Lila calls — " She frowned. "Wait a minute."

"And because I'm Charles' friend," Buddy went

on, "I have a responsibility to tell you that he has a date tonight."

Mrs. Pembroke snapped her fingers. "Goon machine! That's it."

"Listen," Charles muttered. "I can see her another time."

"Oh, sure," Buddy said. "Like Halley's Comet."

"Charles," Mrs. Pembroke said, catching on. "Why don't you just invite her over here?"

"*Here*?"

Buddy threw up his arms in the "Touchdown!" signal, yanking them back before Mrs. Pembroke could see.

"Mrs. Pembroke, no," Charles said uneasily. "You don't want me to do that."

"Why not? It's the least I can do," she said, shrugging. "I ruined your plans."

"But," Charles blinked several times, "she's a *girl*. What — what about the children? They'll see her. They'll *know*."

"The children know everything, Charles," Mrs. Pembroke said wryly. "We have cable."

"But — " Gwendolyn Pierce? On a quiet date at home?

She went over to the phone, handing him the receiver. "Call her."

"Yeah, but — "

They were both looking at him, waiting for him to call.

"It's just — I mean — she's the kind of girl who seems more at home — out."

Mrs. Pembroke went into the kitchen and Buddy sat down at the dining room table.

"And, well," Charles blinked some more. "I promised her a night out, and — " He dialed uncertainly.

"If you want," Buddy said, very generous, "you could set her up with me."

Charles just looked at him, then focused on the phone as a girl answered. "Hello, Gwendolyn? Uh, yeah, this is Charles." He shifted his weight. "Yeah, I was looking forward to seeing you, too —" She *was*? Looking forward to seeing *him*? "But," he went on firmly, "see, the people I work for have to go out and — " And what? "And the children need me, Gwendolyn." Yeah, that was good. "They *need* me." Okay, don't push it. "And I'm sure the last thing you want is to spend a — you'd love to spend a quiet evening at home?" He looked at Buddy who made a victory sign. "Uh, yeah. Ten Barrington Court. Uh, eight-o'clock?" Had she just said yes? "Gwendolyn? Gwendo — " He put the phone down. "She hung up."

Mrs. Pembroke came out of the kitchen. "Everything under control?"

"Uh, yeah. She's coming over here."

"Good," Mrs. Pembroke said, patting him on the shoulder, then starting up the stairs.

"Good," Charles said, much less certain. "Everything's under control." He nodded, more than once, and Buddy laughed.

Since Charles was taking showers, Jason, Douglas, and Lila started dinner without him. As usual, Jason ate his meat and left his vegetables; and Douglas, wearing his rubber alien mask, did the opposite. Lila ignored both of them.

"Look, Douglas," Jason said, gesturing with his fork. "I don't care what Carl Sagan says." He hit the base of the fork on the table. "Soccer is the future."

"Trade you my hamburger for your vegetables," Douglas offered.

Jason sighed as Douglas switched their plates. "Why this time?"

"Because," Douglas lifted a forkful to his mouth, "peas and carrots are living energy from the earth and," he frowned at Jason's plate, "*hamburger* is the charred remains of a *slaughtered* animal carcass."

Lila shuddered, pushing her plate away. "Well, that grosses *me* out for the evening."

Jason put his hands on his hips. "You calling my dinner dead meat?" he asked Douglas.

"No," Charles said, tying his bathrobe belt, fresh from his second shower. "Dead meat is you guys if you ruin my date tonight." Automatically, he lifted Douglas' mask. "I'm having a friend over, okay, and she's a lady."

"*What?*" Douglas said.

Jason grinned. "Female carbon unit."

Douglas nodded, lowering his mask.

"And," Charles went on, "she's not coming over to talk about sports." He cuffed Jason lightly, which made Douglas laugh. "*And*," Charles turned to give him a cuff as well, "she's definitely not coming here to talk Dungeons and Dragons."

"She's *not?*" Jason said, in exaggerated surprise. "Then, why's she coming over?"

"Eat your carcass," Charles said. Lila groaned and covered her ears.

Jason speared a piece of meat, then leaned closer to Douglas, chewing noisily.

"Caveman," Douglas said, disgusted.

"Space mutant."

"Wildebeest!"

"Adopted!" Jason said, his worst and greatest insult.

"Charles!" Douglas said, whipping off his mask.

Charles sighed. "You aren't adopted."

Douglas gave his brother an "I told you so" nod, and lowered his mask to finish his vegetables.

"Then they made a mistake at the hospital," Jason said. "Or he's a test tube baby." He shook his head. "One day I'll figure it out."

Mrs. Pembroke came in, her high heels clicking against the linoleum, putting on gold earrings. "Okay," she said to her sons. "I want you guys on your best behavior tonight. Any questions?"

"Yeah," Jason said. "When Douglas was born, was the circus in town?"

She laughed, patted Douglas on the shoulder, and walked over to the refrigerator, pouring herself a quick glass of iced tea.

Mr. Pembroke walked in, straightening his tie. "Okay," he said to Jason and Douglas. "I want you guys on your best behavior tonight. Any questions?"

"Yeah," Jason said. "When you and Mom were planning Douglas, what exactly did you have in mind?"

Mr. Pembroke coughed, looked at his wife for guidance, and coughed again. "Jason, no questions at the table." He frowned at Lila. "Lila, no playing with your food at the table. Douglas —"

He looked at Douglas, who smiled innocently. "Hi, Douglas."

Lila let her fork fall. "Writing Alexander Morgan in my mashed potatoes isn't playing — it's *worship*."

"Who's Alexander Morgan?" Mr. Pembroke asked. Jason pretended to throw up.

Lila sighed deeply. "Alexander Morgan is *only* the —"

"Class president, best athlete, fabulous-looking, most excellent boy in the eighth grade!" Jason and Douglas chorused. Lila flicked a forkful of mashed potatoes at each.

Mr. Pembroke frowned. "I hate his kind."

Charles laughed.

"And if things work out," Lila said, ignoring all of them, "I'll be popular! I'll be powerful! I'll — I'll be like Eleanor Roosevelt — only *gorgeous*!"

"Never," Jason said.

"When the *glaciers* melt," Douglas said.

"Alexander is coming over tonight so Lila can help him with his homework," Mrs. Pembroke explained.

"Oh." Mr. Pembroke's smile was brave. "Isn't that nice." The smile left, and he pulled Charles over to the back door, lowering his voice. "Charles, I'm thirty-five years old. I'm probably not going to have another little girl. You understand what I'm telling you?"

Charles nodded. "You're telling me that even if this guy *looks* at her wrong, you want me to break his legs."

"Would you do that for me, Charles?"

"Yes, sir."

Mr. Pembroke turned to his wife. "Jill, Charles is turning out to be a very good idea." He nodded to emphasize that, then smiled at Charles. "Well, don't let me interrupt your dinner."

"Oh, not at all," Charles assured him. "In fact, I'm sending out for some Chinese food."

Mr. Pembroke lifted his eyebrows.

"Charles is having company, too," Mrs. Pembroke explained. "Gwendolyn Pierce."

"Oh," Mr. Pembroke said. "Isn't that nice." He pulled Charles back over to the door. "Charles, I'm thirty-five years old. I'm not your father, but you've been with us — how long? Three months?"

Charles nodded.

"I feel I can talk to you," Mr. Pembroke said. "You understand what I'm telling you?"

Charles nodded. "You're telling me that there are young, impressionable children here and I should be careful."

"No," Mr. Pembroke said. "I'm telling you to be careful because," he put his arm around Charles' shoulders, "you're a nice young man, with your whole life in front of you, and the last thing you want to hear right now is — "

"Honey, I'm late," Mrs. Pembroke said.

Mr. Pembroke and Charles looked at each other.

"I think that about says it all, Charles," Mr. Pembroke said.

Chapter Twelve

By eight-o'clock, Charles was *really* nervous. He had changed several times, deciding finally on light gray pants with a matching vest, a pink Madison Avenue Oxford shirt, and a gray-and-pink striped tie. Understated, but cool. He hoped.

Going down to the living room to straighten it one last time, he found Douglas at the coffee table, hunched over his portable Atari.

Charles sighed. "Douglas, what are you doing?"

"Killing Martians," Douglas said cheerfully.

"Killing — " Charles counted to ten. "Well," he said, very pleasantly, "how many do you have to kill?"

"All of them."

"Ah," Charles said. "And, uh, how long will that take?"

Douglas looked solemn, his hand going over his heart. "I've dedicated the rest of my life to it."

"You have, huh?" Charles checked his watch. Eight-oh-one. "Douglas, you want to see how to do it real fast?"

Douglas nodded, intrigued.

Charles yanked the plug out of the socket and the screen went dark. "That's how," he said, and headed for the kitchen.

"That didn't kill them, Charles," Douglas said, very dignified. "That only made them very mad!" He gathered up the set and carried it out of the room.

As Charles lugged a tray with glasses, plates, and silverware out to the living room, the doorbell rang. He jumped, almost dropping the tray.

"Okay, calm," he said. "Calmness." He lowered the tray onto the coffee table. "She's just a girl, and *I* am a mature adult who will not be reduced to a simpering fool." He nodded, and crossed to the door, practicing his greeting. "Hi. Hello. Hi. Simple as that."

The bell rang again.

"Very simple." He opened the door, staring at Gwendolyn who was even more beautiful than usual in a white dress, a light coat draped over her shoulders.

She smiled. "Hello, Charles."

"Hi. Hello. Hi." He smiled weakly. Simple as that.

"Uh, well." Gwendolyn held up a bakery box. "I brought us some dessert — I hope you like it. I wasn't sure what we were having for dinner."

"Chinese," Charles said, relieved. "I was speaking Chinese."

"Oh, I love Chinese food," Gwendolyn said. "And you speak the language?" She took off her coat, obviously impressed.

"Hi-lo," he said, staring at her. "Hiii."

126

"Well, I bet the restaurant was *really* impressed with you." She handed Charles her coat, looking around as he carried it to the closet.

"Okay," Charles said quietly. "Fifteen seconds, and she's still here." He looked down at his hands. "And she can't *go* anywhere because I have her coat!" The possibilities were endless. He started to grin, then shook his head. "There are children in the house. There are *children* in the house." He opened the closet door and Jason grinned up at him. "Jason, get out of there!"

"Okay, okay, just tell me one thing."

"What?" Charles asked impatiently.

"Is there any chance that any of the girls in my school are going to look like that?"

"Jason, all girls are beautiful in their own way." He glanced at Gwendolyn and back. "No." He closed the door, took a deep breath and walked over to the couch. Gwendolyn was already sitting down.

"Here." She handed him a glass of ice water he'd brought out.

"We could have wine," he said, "but the Pembrokes — "

"Ice water's fine," she said, then gestured around the room. "This is a beautiful house. I'd like to live in a house like this someday."

"Oh, yeah, me, too," Charles agreed. "I mean, I do now, but I don't own it. You see, I'd like to own it living in it, if I do, someday — " He shook his head. "Stop it!"

Gwendolyn smiled and lifted her glass. "To a memorable evening."

"Yeah." Charles clinked his glass against hers.

Too hard. "To self-control," he added more quietly.

The doorbell rang again and he jumped up.

"The food!" he said. "I mean, excuse me." He opened the front door, taking out his wallet with his other hand. "Hi. How much do I owe you?"

The boy grinned, holding an algebra book. "How much do you want to give me?"

Charles sighed. "Alexander Morgan."

"Does that mean I don't get any money?" Alexander asked.

Charles turned toward the stairs. "Lila!"

"I'll be right down!" she yelled.

"Come on in," Charles said to Alexander, not noticing the Chinese delivery boy coming up the walk as he shut the door. He started back to the couch, realized that he had just slammed the door in the delivery boy's face, and turned to open it again. "Uh, sorry, pal," he said. "How much?"

The delivery boy smiled and bowed, his Yankees' cap bobbing.

"Twenty-eight dollah."

Charles stared at him, then at the two bags. "Twenty-eight dollar? For what, twenty-eight dollar?"

"You order four dishie."

"No, I didn't. I ordered *two* dishes."

"Something wrong, Charles?" Gwendolyn asked from the couch.

"Oh, no," he said. "No, no, everything's fine. Just a little misunderstanding, that's all."

"Oh. Why don't you explain it to him in Chinese?" she suggested.

Charles looked at her to see if she was serious, couldn't tell, and looked at the delivery boy. "I order two dishie!" he said, in heavy dialect.

"Hey, look, pal," the delivery boy said, his accent gone. "I'm just trying to make a living, so don't hassle me. Comprende?"

Lila walked elegantly down the stairs, her hair up, makeup perfect, beautiful in a green silk dress. "I see our dinner's arrived," she said, her voice almost as elegant as her pose.

"Lila?" Charles said, stunned.

"Lila?" Alexander said, more stunned.

"Rira?" the delivery boy asked.

Charles looked at him.

"Sorry," the delivery boy said, shrugging. "Couldn't resist."

Lila took one of the bags from Charles. "Thank you."

"What are you trying to do to me?" he asked, low enough so that Alexander and Gwendolyn wouldn't hear. "I can't afford twenty-eight dollars for food."

She glanced at Alexander, then sighed. "I'll type your next paper."

"Deal," Charles said.

"Come on, Alex," Lila said, speaking normally. "We'll study up in my room."

Charles watched them go halfway up the stairs before recovering himself. "Hey! You will not! You'll study down here in the living room!"

"Can't," Lila said sweetly. "The books are in my room."

"Yeah, but —"

"Come on, Charles," Gwendolyn said, taking the other bag of food from him. "*We'll* study in the living room."

"No, Gwendolyn, I — "

"We'll study chicken lo mein by the firelight," she said.

He paused on his way up the stairs. "Yeah? But — " He turned towards Lila's room. "Lila!" he hissed. "Lila, I want you down *here*."

"Charles," Gwendolyn said and as he turned, smiled at him. "Come get it while it's hot."

He smiled weakly. "I — " He started down the stairs. "I mean, I — "

Douglas came out of Charles' bedroom, wearing his space mutant mask. "The rebels are taken!" he said, his voice evil and triumphant. "Mars is *mine!*" He strode to the kitchen, fists clenched in front of him.

Charles watched him go, looked at Gwendolyn, then sank onto the stairs. "It's possible I'm losing control," he said.

It was later, the food was gone, and Charles and Gwendolyn sat a couple of feet apart on the couch, Charles staring straight ahead with his elbows on his knees.

"Charles, you haven't been paying very much attention to me this evening," she said mildly.

"You're right," he said, straightening up. "I'm sorry."

"Oh, don't be." Her grin was wry. "This has never happened to me before — I'm beginning to feel refreshingly insecure." She moved closer, touching his forehead with one hand. "Now,

130

Charles, what's going on up there?"

He stood abruptly, scowling upstairs. "She's got a guy alone in her room. *That's* what's going on up there."

"Well," Gwendolyn said. "You've got a girl alone down here. You're even."

Charles let out his breath. Gwendolyn Pierce, the goddess of Crawford College, was flirting with him and he was too worried to pay attention. Unbelievable. "You don't understand, Gwendolyn — I'm being paid to break his legs." Remembering that, he ran halfway up the stairs. "Lila? I want that door open! Now!"

"We're busy in here!" she shouted from her room.

Busy? Mr. Pembroke was going to kill him. "What are you busy doing?" he demanded.

"The door's unlocked," she said. "You can come upstairs and see."

Charles continued up the stairs, Lila coming out to the landing.

"*But*, if you do," she said, "you'll betray my confidence and I'll hate you forever. *Or* you can go back downstairs to your date where you belong and I'll continue to have my tiny crush on you." She paused for effect. "Our entire relationship hinges on this *one* moment, Charles."

He stopped, considering that.

"Your move," Gwendolyn said behind him.

He turned to see her standing with her arms folded, Lila standing with *her* arms folded, and gave up, walking downstairs to the closet. He opened the door and looked down at Jason, who was still in there.

"I'm dead here," he said. "Because on the one hand, if I barge in, I represent the adult and then I relinquish my own hold on childhood to become the authority figure."

Jason nodded.

"Right," Charles said. "Then, once that happens, I'll start to get old. Become preoccupied with *income* tax. Listen to all-news stations on the car radio. . . . " He shuddered. "But, on the other hand — "

"On the other hand," Jason said, "you have a date who wonders why you're talking to a closet."

Remembering, Charles turned to see Gwendolyn watching him, arms still folded. "Hello. Hiii," he said.

Jason stepped out of the closet, holding out his hand. "Jason Pembroke," he said to Gwendolyn.

She smiled and shook it. "Gwendolyn Pierce."

"*I'll* say."

"You know, I have a little brother just like you." She looked up. "Charles, I think this is the first time I've been homesick since I've been at school."

"Jason, you're making the girl sick," Charles said. "Get outta here."

Jason grinned and sat at the dining room table.

"Charles, you know what we should do?" Gwendolyn said.

He took her hand, leading her back to the couch. "What we should do, is listen to me tell you how your eyes shine by the firelight."

Jason gagged.

"No," Gwendolyn said, but looked at Charles shyly. "Yeah?"

"Yeah," he said, back to the Buddy Lembeck

School of Suave. "I could probably talk about your eyes for the rest of our natural lives."

"No, you couldn't," she said demurely.

"Oh, yes," Charles said, completely in control now, "I — "

"Look, lady," Jason interrupted. "He spent forty minutes just standing in front of the mirror for you. You *owe* him!"

"Oh, boy," Charles said and put his head in his hands.

"Charles!" Gwendolyn's hands went onto her hips.

"Jason," he said. "I want you to sit outside Lila's bedroom door and tell me what happens every five minutes, you got that?" He looked at Gwendolyn smiling at him. "Uh, make that ten minutes."

Jason stepped back as though affronted. "You mean you want me to *spy* on my own sister?"

"Yes."

Jason's eyes lit up. "Thanks, Charles!" He took the stairs three at a time. "Spy on my own sister? I love you, Charles!"

Lila played with her cassette deck, trying to find a romantic tape, rejecting Culture Club, Loverboy, and Duran Duran in rapid succession. She settled on the Police and turned to look at Alexander, who was sitting on the floor, absorbed by their algebra homework.

He looked up at her. "Two equals x to the fourth power," he said uncertainly.

"Not even close."

"Fifth power?" He sighed, rubbing one hand

across his forehead. "Lila, I really can't concentrate with this music."

"Don't you like this song?" she asked, swaying slightly to the beat. "I think it's very romantic."

"Why does two have to equal x?" he asked. "Why do numbers have to equal letters? I never hurt anybody!"

"Alex —"

"X equals — negative twelve square cubed a million percent?"

Lila shook her head. Some seduction *this* was. "You're just guessing."

"Well, I don't get it." He scowled at the page of equations. "What's the nature of x? What is the very *essence* of x? What —"

"Will you forget about x already?" Lila yelled. "You'll have a nervous breakdown over it! X isn't going to help you in life, unless you're playing Scrabble — and even then, it's only worth eight points!" Alexander was staring at her and she sank onto the bed, completely frustrated. "Eight lousy points."

Downstairs, Charles watched Gwendolyn's eyes shine in the firelight for a while, then leaned forward to kiss her. They moved closer together, still kissing; then, she jumped up.

"You kissed me!" she said.

"Well, yeah." Charles looked at her, then at the empty place on the couch where he had just been kissing someone. "And you kissed me back!"

"Friendly," Gwendolyn said. "I kissed you *friendly*, Charles." She pointed an accusing finger at him. "You *meant* your kiss." She strode across the room to the closet to get her coat.

"Yeah, I meant my kiss," he said, confused. "I always mean my kisses! I mean, except for this aunt I had who — "

"You really had me going," Gwendolyn said, hand on the closet door. "With all your charm and your modesty and this cute little house of yours — you probably rented the kids just to throw me off guard, right?"

Nervously, Charles ran his hand back through his hair. "Gwendolyn, what is it? Was it a bad kiss? You can tell me — I'm not proud."

Gwendolyn's expression was not amused.

Okay, okay, keep going. Buddy would keep going. "I have one kiss," he said. "If it's no good, teach me. Here." He turned his cheek to her. "Use my face."

She shoved him, much stronger than he would have imagined, and he stumbled backward, falling over the couch and landing on the floor. Gwendolyn stormed over to the closet and yanked the door open. Douglas, wearing his mutant mask and standing where Jason had been, held up her coat.

"Thank you," Gwendolyn said shortly and left, slamming the front door behind her.

Douglas lifted his Atari from the closet floor and carried it over to the couch. "Early evening, huh, Charles?"

Charles groaned.

"Now, if you'll excuse me," Douglas said, setting the game down on the coffee table and plugging it in, "I'll be invading Venus."

As he started to play, the front door flew open and Gwendolyn strode back in.

"There's nothing wrong with the way you kiss," she said. "That's beside the point!"

Charles looked up blearily, realized that she was back, and yanked the plug out of the video game.

"A planet," Douglas said, looking at the dark screen. "A whole planet. Gone." He walked upstairs, shaking his head.

"The point is," Gwendolyn continued when Douglas was gone, "that every creep I go out with tries, and I can't stand it anymore!" She let out her breath, anger fading. "You know, I wanted to come over here tonight because you seemed different. Sincere."

So, what else was new? "Do *not* call me sincere," Charles said through his teeth. "Okay? Everybody calls me sincere! And you haven't known me long enough to call me sincere!"

"Well, I happen to think that it's a very attractive part of you," Gwendolyn said. "If you could bottle it, you'd make a fortune!"

Charles looked at her, hands on his hips, out of breath. "Yeah, you think so, huh?"

"Yeah," she said.

"Yeah, well, I wouldn't." He resisted a strong urge to kick the chair next to him. *Hard.* "I'd only break even because I've already spent eight hundred thousand dollars on Wild Musk!" Now, he *did* kick the chair leg. "Sincere. Hah!"

"Yeah," Gwendolyn said. "Sincere."

He sighed. He *was* sincere. What a curse. "Okay, okay, I admit it," he said. "I'm a sincere guy! Okay? And what about you? Gwendolyn Pierce the beautiful! Gwendolyn Pierce the superb!" He sighed an exaggeratedly deep sigh. "I'll tell you something. The reason I didn't want you to come over tonight is because a lot of times I'm not exactly sure how sincere I am!"

"Yeah, well," Gwendolyn said, "a lot of times I'm not sure how Gwendolyn Pierce I am either!"

That remark was unexpected and he forgot about sincerity. "What do you mean?"

"I mean, *I've* heard all about me, too, Charles, and sometimes I don't even *want* to be Gwendolyn Pierce."

Charles thought about that. "But — someone has to."

"Hey, Charles," Jason said from the landing.

"What."

"It's ten minutes."

Naturally. Charles closed his eyes. "Tell me what's going on up there, Jason, and make it fast."

"Okay." Jason did a quick push-up against the railing, remembering. "The last thing he said was, 'Come on, Lila, you know why I came here tonight. Why are you playing games with me?'"

Charles nodded. "Fine, Jason. Good job. Thank you." He turned back to Gwendolyn. "Look, the point I'm —" He stopped, realizing what Jason had just said, and ran up the stairs. When Mr. Pembroke came home, he was going to be dog food.

"Look, Lila," Alexander was saying inside her room. "I can get this from someone else, you know. So, if I'm wasting my time here, tell me and I'll leave."

Charles burst into the room, heading straight for the bed. "Let him leave, Lila! You don't need

137

him for a boy —" He stopped, seeing that they were sitting on opposite sides of the room; Lila slouched on her windowseat, Alexander holding his math book. "— friend," he said lamely.

"*Boy*friend?" Alexander said.

"Thanks a lot, Charles." Lila stood up, pushing past him and out of the room; Gwendolyn went after her.

Charles sat down on the bed, putting his head in his hands.

"Charles?" Jason asked, grinning.

Charles didn't lift his head. "What."

"Is this what happens when boys start talking to girls?"

"Mmmm," Charles said.

Jason patted him on the back, and walked out to the hall, leaving Charles and Alexander alone.

Slowly, Alexander closed his book. "I didn't know she felt that way about me."

Charles lifted his head. "I thought you were the most excellent boy in the eighth grade."

"Yeah." Alexander slumped down. "It's a curse."

Charles blinked. "What?" Seemed he was hearing that a lot lately.

"Sure," Alexander said unhappily. "The girls in the class made me popular, but they're more comfortable talking *about* me than *to* me." He slumped lower. "I'm not a person — I'm a contest."

Charles looked at the most excellent boy in the eighth grade, thought about Gwendolyn the beautiful, thought about Mr. Sincere. "Huh," he said.

*   *   *

"I don't believe it," Lila said, pacing behind the couch. "He actually wanted to do *homework*. He came into my house. We were alone in my room. And *that's* what he actually wanted to do." Seeing Gwendolyn smile, Lila sat on the couch next to her. "Guess this never happens to *you*, huh?"

"No." Gwendolyn grinned wryly. "No, I don't get too many calls for homework." She paused. "I wish I did."

"How come?"

"Because that would mean I was respected as a thinking person."

"That's so important?"

"Only when you're not," Gwendolyn said quietly.

"But — " Lila frowned, digesting all of this. "He's Alexander Morgan! I'm supposed to think of him as the most excellent —"

"No, you're not," Charles said, on his way down the stairs with Alexander. He grabbed Gwendolyn's hand, dragging her to the kitchen.

"Charles!" She tried to pull free. "What are you —"

"I have to tell you something," he said, holding both of her hands as the kitchen door swung shut. "I've been a wreck all day about this date. Because you weren't a *person*."

She didn't say anything, waiting for him to go on.

"You were a name! And a sigh!" He indicated an imaginary girl walking by. "Oh, look, there goes Gwendolyn Pierce!" He sighed deeply, then looked serious again. "But you have to understand something. Once you walked through that door, I watched *you*. And I listened to *you*, and you became real, and it wasn't Gwendolyn Pierce I kissed — it was you! Because I like you." He stopped, taking a deep breath before going on. "And just because you happen to be Gwendolyn Pierce isn't going to stop me from kissing you again!" He kissed her, and slowly, they moved apart.

"You really mean all that?" she asked.

He grinned. "Sincerely."

They smiled at each other and walked back into the living room, Charles keeping his hand on her waist. Alexander was sitting on the arm of the couch, next to Lila.

"How about this," he was saying. "X equals you and I should go for ice cream."

"Good answer," Lila said, standing up.

"Uh, look, Lila." Charles moved over to put his arm around her. "Your father is thirty-five years old. It's quarter after nine, and he probably isn't going to have any more daughters. You understand what I'm telling you?"

Lila nodded reluctantly. "You're telling me it's too late to go out."

"No, I'm not." He winked at Gwendolyn across the room. "I'm just telling you that we have to come along."

"You and Gwendolyn?" Lila asked, and Charles nodded. "I like Gwendolyn! I respect her as a thinking person!"

Gwendolyn laughed.

"Hey!" Douglas said, running down the stairs

in his astronaut suit. "Did I hear someone say ice cream?"

"Girls can wait," Jason said, right behind him. He yanked the front door open just as Mr. and Mrs. Pembroke, home early, started to open it from the outside.

"Hey," Mr. Pembroke said, keys in midair. "Where's everyone —"

"Ice cream!" Jason said, running outside.

"Lots of ice cream!" Douglas said, going out after him.

"Major amounts," Lila agreed, right behind them.

"Hello," Alexander said politely, following Lila.

"It's very nice to meet you," Gwendolyn added, shaking each parent's hand in turn.

"— going?" Mr. Pembroke finished, even though everyone except Charles was gone.

"Care to join us?" Charles asked.

"Yeah," Mrs. Pembroke said. "That sounds like a good —"

"We'll pass," Mr. Pembroke interrupted.

Mrs. Pembroke looked at him blankly. "We will?"

"And take your time," Mr. Pembroke said, clapping Charles on the back. "I'm not worried as long as you're in charge."

"Well." Charles coughed, the clap on the back pretty hard. "Thank you, sir." He nodded at Mrs. Pembroke. "Good-night."

As Charles left, Mr. Pembroke closed the door, looking significantly at his wife.

"The house is empty, Jill," he said. "There's nobody home. Do you understand what I'm telling you?"

Mrs. Pembroke nodded. "You're telling me —" She stopped, catching on to what he was telling her, and they smiled at each other.

"There are no *children* in the house!" they said together, moving into an embrace.

Outside, Charles checked his wallet, decided that he might need more money, and put his hand on the doorknob.

"Charles is turning out to be a very good idea," Mr. Pembroke was saying.

"Mmmm," Mrs. Pembroke was saying, and it was quiet.

Charles smiled, turning away from the door. "I can't help it," he said to the mailbox and jogged to catch up with Gwendolyn and the others.